Matchmakers o...

Sisters Eleanor and Mary St. Aubin and their
old school friend Lady Henrietta Briggs have
used their combined wit, social connections and
determination to create a living for themselves
as professional matchmakers.

The St. Aubin and Briggs Confidential Agency in
Bath prides itself on discreetly matching ladies
and gentlemen in need of a marriage partner.

In *The Earl's Cinderella Countess*,
Eleanor is heartbroken to discover that their
new client is the Earl of Fleetwood—her childhood
friend and first love. Can Ella set aside her feelings
and find Frederick a suitable heiress to wed?

Look out for the next book

Coming soon!

The Earl's
Cinderella Countess

———

AMANDA McCABE

Recycling programs
for this product may
not exist in your area.

ISBN-13: 978-1-335-59607-9

The Earl's Cinderella Countess

Copyright © 2024 by Ammanda McCabe

Harlequin Enterprises ULC
22 Adelaide St. West, 41st Floor
Toronto, Ontario M5H 4E3, Canada
www.Harlequin.com

Printed in U.S.A.

Amanda McCabe wrote her first romance at sixteen—a vast historical epic starring all her friends as the characters, written secretly during algebra class! She's never since used algebra, but her books have been nominated for many awards, including the RITA® Award, Booksellers' Best Award, National Readers' Choice Award and the HOLT Medallion. In her spare time she loves taking dance classes and collecting travel souvenirs. Amanda lives in New Mexico. Visit her at ammandamccabe.com.

Books by Amanda McCabe

Harlequin Historical

Betrayed by His Kiss
The Demure Miss Manning
The Queen's Christmas Summons
"His Mistletoe Lady"
in *Tudor Christmas Tidings*
A Manhattan Heiress in Paris
"A Convenient Winter Wedding"
in *A Gilded Age Christmas*

Debutantes in Paris

Secrets of a Wallflower
The Governess's Convenient Marriage
Miss Fortescue's Protector in Paris

Dollar Duchesses

His Unlikely Duchess
Playing the Duke's Fiancée
Winning Back His Duchess

Visit the Author Profile page
at Harlequin.com for more titles.

Prologue

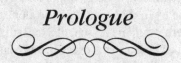

For love is a celestial harmony
Of likely hearts compos'd of stars' concent,
Which join together in sweet sympathy,
To work each other's joy and true content
—Edmund Spenser

1808

'*I'm afraid you cannot return to school in the New Year, Eleanor dearest. With your mother sadly gone, there is so much for you to do here at the vicarage. I do so rely on your good sense...*'

Eleanor St Aubin could hardly bear it another moment. Could hardly bear the walls of the old vicarage, whitewashed and hung with gloomy old paintings, the sound of her father humming to himself as he wrote his sermon in his library, where he stayed almost all the time. *Humming!* As if he hadn't just brought her world—what was left of her world after losing dear Mama—around her very ears.

She'd clung to the idea of going back to Mrs Meecham's School for Clergymen's Daughters in the bustle and colour of Bath, with her sister Mary. Clung to the thought that soon she would be with her friends, her books and her music lessons, walks across the hills and parks of the town. She would not be alone.

Now there would be no school. No Bath or music or friends. Papa needed a housekeeper, and Mary was only ten, no use at all. She would go back to school. Eleanor was fourteen and 'sensible'. So she would stay home.

Eleanor stood in the middle of the small drawing room, among her mother's dark-green-cushioned furniture and the scent of beeswax polish, woodsmoke and tea cakes, which she would now be responsible for providing. She listened to her father's humming and the thud of his books as he stacked them on his desk. She could hear the cook in the kitchen, clanging pots and pans, and imagined she also heard her chores in the still-room, the jam and potpourri and herbs calling to her. She imagined the parade of parishioners coming endlessly to their door, through the tangled garden pathway that also needed her urgent attention. They would want tea and cakes and would need placating as they waited for her father, who was always late.

Eleanor sighed. She didn't mind talking to the parishioners, really, even when it was about dull altar flowers and fetes to raise coin for the roof. In fact, she quite enjoyed that part, the organising and helping and the solving of problems.

Mama had been so splendid at it all, the church matters *and* the housekeeping. Chatting with people and bringing a tea tray in once in a while.

Eleanor's old chores were far from those she had being the lady of the vicarage and she already felt as if she was drowning. She had no idea how to do any of it! No idea how to manage their few servants, see to meals, tidy the garden and be gracious and smiling all the time.

She'd always half imagined that she might one day marry a curate herself and keep her own vicarage just as Mama had. But that was in some hazy 'someday', when she was older, more learned and not so very awkward and unsure. Not now, when she was still a schoolgirl.

Her frantic stare fell on a barley twist side table, its books and porcelain vases covered with a film of dust. Without her mother's close eye on every detail, things were descending into chaos. And now Eleanor was the one who had to pay the attention.

She closed her eyes against the dust. Against the windows that needed washing and the curtains that needed mending. She did not *want* to be the grown-up! She wanted to go back to school, to the pale houses and crowded streets of Bath. She wanted a little more time to decipher out her life, not have it thrust upon her without her say-so. She wanted to cry and kick something and rail about unfairness! She wanted…

She wanted her mother. That was what she wanted. She wanted Mary Ellen St Aubin to hug her close and tell her all would be well. But it would not. Not now.

'Eleanor,' her father called out plaintively. 'Have you seen my spectacles?'

The cook shouted at the scullery maid and Mary

shrieked from her chamber upstairs. Eleanor couldn't bear it another moment. The chaos *she* was meant to control now, the absence of Mama, the realisation that this was her every day now and there was no escape—she was suffocating.

She spun around and raced out of the drawing room, through the small, flagstone-floored foyer, and yanked the door open. Luckily, there was no one on the pathway, no poor soul seeking solace from the vicar and tea and cakes from the housekeeper—from her. She heard a hum of conversation from the churchyard just beyond the garden hedge, but she couldn't see anyone. She clutched at handfuls of her grey muslin skirt and ran. She ran down the overgrown path, veering a bit towards the church, its old Norman stone tower stretching towards the cloudy sky as if it watched her. She dashed through the lych-gate into the lane.

She didn't stop running.

Rather than head towards the village, a small but pretty place lined with shops, where everyone knew her and where someone was bound to see her and report her hoydenish behaviour to her father, she went to the woods that stretched in the opposite direction, cool and green and quiet.

The woods were part of the estate at Moulton Magna, the grand property of the Earl of Fleetwood, the greatest lord in the neighbourhood. Since the Earl was friends with her father, indeed had bestowed on him the living in the first place, no one in the Canning family—the Earl, Countess and their sons, plus a vast staff—cared when the vicar and his daughters walked there. It was a beautiful spot, with groves and streams, smelling of the fresh, green air and Eleanor usually loved it.

She enjoyed the company of the Canning brothers, as well, she had to admit. Especially the younger, Lord Frederick, he of the glowing sky-blue eyes and easy laughter. His teasing ways that made her blush and stammer, made her close her eyes and picture him at night and wish she had said something different to him, been someone different. She always sought him out there when they were both home from school, even if she told herself she did not.

But today she hoped she wouldn't see Fred, or any of them. She could feel drops of moisture at her temples from her mad dash, dampening her dark brown hair. Curls escaped their pins and clung to her neck, and she was sure her eyes must be red from crying, her pale cheeks blotchy. She would be a terrible sight, a disgrace to the vicarage. And she couldn't bear for Fred, of all people, to see her that way! To tease her and laugh at her, even in his light, joking way. She didn't want him to remember her that way.

She saw no one as she ran down a winding, mossy path, towards a small summerhouse that topped a rolling rise. It had long been a favourite spot for her, as well as for Mary and the Canning brothers. The view from its colonnaded portal stretched for miles—meadows and trees and the grand, glowing house of Moulton Magna. They would chase each other there, laughing and teasing. Today, she wanted to be alone. To not have to be the strong, sensible one everyone said she was. She had the rest of her life to do that.

She stumbled up the steps of the little, round, domed building and into the single room. Greyish sunlight filtered through the skylight high overhead, dappling the dried leaves that drifted over the mosaic floor, reminding her that autumn was lengthening and when winter came she wouldn't be at school. She'd be here. Alone in the summerhouse, which echoed now with old laughter.

She sat down on a wrought iron chaise, its cushions taken inside now. She didn't feel the hard press of the bare slats, though, or the chill of the marble walls. She let that silence wrap around her and drew her knees up to press her forehead against them. The tears fell then, until she had no more of them. There was only a sort of tired resignation.

She wanted to blame Papa, to curse at him, even though she couldn't. It was not his fault, not really. Her mother had been so superb at her job of keeping the vicarage and he couldn't begin to do all she had done. He didn't know how, and he had his own tasks of sermon-writing and consoling the bereaved, comforting the dying, celebrating marriages and new babies. She was the female. She had to cook and clean and manage servants. It was how the world worked. She was the eldest daughter. The duties were hers, along with helping Mary, and they had to be done.

But, oh! She had loved school and her friends and books. Loved Bath, glowing like honey in the light, the Avon bubbling past, laughter and people and shops.

She reached under the chaise and found the basket

of books she'd left there still waiting. Novels and poetry—things not suitable for the vicarage library. She took out her favourite, Spenser's *The Fairy Queen,* with its etched illustrations of the Redcrosse Knight and his true love Una.

The door cracked open, letting in a bar of light and a breeze that stirred at the leaves. Her stomach lurched as she was suddenly dragged out of her fantasy world. She dropped her feet to the floor and wiped at her damp cheeks. Had her father caught her? She didn't want him to feel even worse! Didn't want to put her tears on anyone else.

But it was not her father or sister, or a Canning gamekeeper come to lecture her against racing through the park. It was Fred. The last person she wanted to see. The only person she wanted to see.

He stood there in the doorway, half in the wavering shadows, and studied her with a worried frown. Eleanor felt her tense shoulders ease at just his presence and she clutched the book close to her with a sigh.

Fred, though he was much older than her at nineteen, and *very* handsome indeed, with his waves of amber-gold hair and sharp cheekbones, his bright blue eyes filled with laughter was much sought after by every eligible young lady within miles and miles, had always been such a friend to her.

There was the flash of a deep dimple when he smiled at her. He spoke to her not as if she was a silly child or a sensible housekeeper, but as a lady who understood poetry and history and who loved to run and dance even when she shouldn't. He raced her through the woods, taught her the rules of cricket, read with her, teased her, laughed with her. He was always quick to make her giggle when life at the vicarage was too dour, to run with her, read poetry with her, tell her tales of the world outside.

Yes—he was her friend. And if, in the quiet of her dark chamber at night, she dared to dream he might be more, might one day kiss her and hold her close—well, that was *her* secret. She knew he never would, not really. He was handsome as a god, as a prince in a poem, and the son of an earl. But the dreams were so lovely.

'Ella,' he said softly, kindly. 'Are you unwell? I was riding by and saw you running.'

Eleanor ducked her head, hoping he wouldn't see those red eyes and splotched cheeks. She was plain enough in comparison to him already! 'I—I'm all right, Fred, really. I just—my father told me I cannot return to school. He needs my help at the vicarage.'

'Oh, Ella. I am sorry,' he said.

His voice was full of sympathy and understanding and she feared it would make her cry all over again. He was one of the few who knew how much she really loved it at school, for she confided in him about her friends and studies. They read *The Fairy Queen* together while he told her about his own school and his hopes for the future away from his own family.

He gestured at the book she clutched. 'You could be Una.'

She felt her lips tug at a reluctant smile, even though she knew he flattered her just to cheer her up. 'And you shall always be the *parfit gentil knight*. The Red-crosse Knight.'

He smiled in return, but Eleanor sensed something rather sad and dark in the gesture. Something not like Fred, who was always so merry and ready to run and laugh.

She sat up straighter. 'Is something amiss?'

'Of course not. It's just…' He stepped closer, into the glow from the skylight. He wore a red coat, glittering with touches of gold.

'Fred…' she whispered, a cold knot forming in her stomach. 'Are you— That is…'

'I'm also leaving, yes. I have my commission in the Grenadiers and we're leaving for the Peninsula tomorrow. I was looking for you to say…'

'To say goodbye?' she choked out. Her eyes prickled and she warned herself sternly not to start crying again.

She had long known Fred was meant for the Army. His older brother, the dashing Henry, was the heir to Moulton Magna. Their destinies sorted them as surely as hers did for her and Mary. Fred would surely go far in the Army, flourish there where his bravery and gift for friendship would be valued and she was happy for him.

But—oh! He was one more loss, after her mother and her school and any foolish hopes she might have dared harbour about the future. That one day a miracle would happen and Fred could be hers, even though he was the Earl's son and she the vicar's daughter.

She rose slowly to her feet and took a step closer to him. He smelled wonderfully of sunshine and lemon soap and just *Fred*. She was suddenly achingly aware this could be the last time she saw him. It was certainly the last time she would see *this* Fred and be *this* Eleanor. So many images scrolled through her mind in a great flash—his smile, the blue glow of his eyes, the freedom of laughing with him.

She gently touched his hand. It was warm and slightly rough, so alive under her fingers, and she longed to clutch at him, hold on to him and this moment for always.

'I shall miss you,' she said simply. She could think of no other words.

He smiled at her, a flash of his old teasing grin, and turned his hand to hold onto hers. 'And I will miss you, Ella. Will you keep the book for me? Think of me adventuring when you read it?'

She gave him another smile in answer. It felt rather watery, weak, but she yearned to put all she felt into it. All she thought of him in her secret heart. All she hoped for him. She couldn't bear to send him off with a vision of red eyes and miserable weeping! 'Of course I shall. No one could ever read the lines as you do, though. Really, you should have been one to tread the boards rather than march in the Army!'

'I'm glad your father is here to keep an eye on Moulton Magna for me. I have the feeling my parents and brother will need all the prayers they can find!'

Eleanor shook her head, thinking of the Earl, of Henry and their carelessness. But it was Fred who would be in danger. She had the gnawing, anxious sense that it was Fred who needed the prayers, needed someone to look after him. And it could not be her.

To her horror, she felt those tears well in her eyes again.

'Oh, Ella,' he said, his sharply carved face crumpling in worry. 'Don't cry, please! I can stand anyone crying, but not you.'

'Because I am sensible and strong?' she whispered.

'You are that. But also because of your dear heart, your laughter and poetry. Your kindness. No one is kinder than you, Ella. I need you to keep watch for me here. You're the only one I can really count on.'

Eleanor nodded, cherishing those words. Trying to remember them for the long days ahead. But she hated the hint of worry in his voice, the tinge of some foreboding, and it made her shiver. She longed to cling onto him even closer, to not to let him leave her side. 'You *can* rely on me, Fred. I'll be—thinking about you a great deal and sending you all best wishes wherever you are.' Sending him her heart, even though he would never know it.

He gently touched her cheek, tracing the last of her tears. 'So, friends always, Ella?'

Friends. Such a pale word for what she felt for him, for her secret dreams. But it was a precious gift nonetheless. One she hugged close. 'Yes. The best of friends.'

To her shock, he took her hand in his, holding it tight and bent his head to press a soft, gentle kiss to her fingers. Then he turned and left and she was alone again.

Eleanor curled her fingers tight, as if she could hold

on to that kiss. The thrilling sensation of it all. The bright, sunshiny tingles. She wanted to remember it always, remember *him*.

She smoothed out his handkerchief, running her fingertip over the embroidered blue *FC*. She fancied she could smell his lemony soap there, the essence of Fred and his golden glow.

'The best of friends,' she whispered. She folded up the handkerchief carefully, tucked it in the pages of the book and stepped back out into the real world to face the future, carrying with her the memory of Fred and his kiss.

Chapter One

Late 1816

'And so that is it?' Fred asked the dour-faced lawyer who sat across the desk from Fred and Penelope, his father's widow. He could hardly absorb what the man was saying in his quiet, steady, solemn, oh-so-matter-of-fact voice.

Fred had seen much in his years in the Army, culminating in the hell of Waterloo. He had seen mud and blood and misery, biting cold and brutal sun. He had seen friends killed and maimed. He bore his own scars. A face lined with red wounds and a weakened hand. Sometimes all that had sustained him then was the memory of his 'Una', Eleanor St Aubin, and her sweet smiles.

Yet he never imagined he would return to all this.

His father had never been a man who loved, or could be loved, especially once Fred's mother died and all the softness and kindness and order of Moulton Magna went with her. And his brother had always cared only for hunting and fishing, not about the fact that one day he would be the Earl. Now they were both gone and Fred was the Earl himself. All the misery and death that he'd seen in battle had followed him, even to this peaceful place, and clung to him like a ghost. There was no time to grieve as he should. The estate and all who depended on it were his responsibility. He had to do his very best for them.

And now this. Not only was Moulton Magna his now—so were its debts. They were most considerable. For it seemed his father had enjoyed gambling while Fred was gone. Any sense of duty had been lost on the card tables.

For one long moment, he could say nothing else. Thoughts raced one after another through his mind, chasing and spiralling. How could this have happened? How had his father and brother been so far gone? All Fred knew was the Army. Yet now he had to fix this debacle. He had learned how to be a soldier, how to keep calm in the midst of battle, but this was something else entirely. This was something he never expected. Another kind of chaos.

He glanced at Penelope, sitting beside him in her inky veils. She looked deeply sad, but not surprised. Then again, she had lived in the crumbling house at Moulton Magna for years while Fred was away so much. Pen was young. She'd been married off by her family after her first husband died suddenly. No doubt when they thought an earl would offer her security. Now she, too, was adrift.

She gave him a quick, sweet smile, as if she tried to reassure him. His father had not deserved her, with her kind nature, her gentle humour and her pretty face. She'd been a good friend to Fred.

'Pen...' he began.

She reached out with her black-gloved hand to touch his arm.

'Oh, Fred, please don't worry about me,' she murmured. 'I know this is a such a shock. Your father...'

The lawyer cleared his throat. 'Indeed, Lord Fleetwood. I have here a list of the late earl's debts and a few of the assets of the estate. The estate manager will certainly have more detailed information for you. I suggest his lordship was not, er, entirely well in his final years.'

Penelope gave a little snort behind her black-edged handkerchief. His father never had been the most responsible of men, even before Fred left, but according to servants' tales he had grown far worse once Fred had gone. And Pen had had to deal with all that.

'But Lady Fleetwood does have her jointure, which cannot be touched,' the lawyer said. 'As well as a small sum from her own family.'

'I shall find a small place for myself, Fred. Perhaps in Bath, or someplace like that,' Penelope said. 'I will be quite well. Much better, in fact.'

Fred smiled at her. That was one good thing. Penelope did deserve a happy life now.

'I can help you,' she said.

He shook his head. 'No. You have helped enough. Too much.'

And she had. The people of Moulton Magna loved

her, even though his father had neglected them shamefully. It was Fred's job to see them all right now. No matter what it took.

Chapter Two

Bath, 1817

'I need a wife. The best! You must find her for me. Immediately.'

Eleanor exchanged a quick glance with her sister Mary and bit her lip to keep from bursting into laughter. Even Miss Muffins, their little terrier puppy, propped on her velvet cushion beneath the desk, looked startled by their potential new patron. Mary widened her pretty grass-green eyes, mouthed *Immediately!* and Eleanor shuffled a few papers about before she dared look back at Mr Higgleston-Worth.

The St Aubin and Briggs Confidential Agency was a most discreet, discerning and, it had to be said, successful place, where people who desired to be married but perhaps had a small difficulty or two could come for advice.

However, the agency didn't always attract easy-to-place clients. Oh, no. People who were easy to match had no need of their service. People who were handsome, pleasant and wealthy were not St Aubin and

Briggs' usual bread and butter. They had acquired a fine reputation for, so to say, finding a lid for every pot. The shy, the outwardly abrasive but inwardly insecure, the older and younger and plainer and choosier. Those were the people who came to the agency.

St Aubin and Briggs found fine marriages for them all—well, most of them—and their files were filled with grateful letters from those now ensconced in marital bliss.

Eleanor had learned in their work to never be daunted. Since she and Mary had opened their office with their old school friend Henrietta, the widowed Lady Briggs, they had found great success, beyond their modest hopes. When Papa had died and they'd had to leave the vicarage, the home they'd known all their lives, they'd been thrown into frantic worry. Their only choice had seemed to be separating from each other, going out as governesses or ladies' companions. Scraping by in a cold, lonely world. Until Harry had come to the rescue.

'I have my little bit of jointure,' she'd said as she had helped them pack up their meagre belongings. *'And a fine new house in Bath! No more dull country days for me.'*

'Bath…' Mary had sighed dreamily, as she'd often tended to be. *'I do long for Bath again!'*

Eleanor had laughed. *'School was delightful there, Mary darling, but after we last went there with Papa to take the waters, you declared you would scream if you saw one more wheeled, wicker chair!'*

Mary had bitten her lip, shaken her golden curls

and tossed a large volume of sermons into the 'to be sold' crate.

'That is only because we spent too much time in doctors' premises to have any fun! Poor Papa. But there could be dances and theatres, assemblies, garden parties. If only...'

'Then you must come with me,' Harry had declared.

She'd always been their leader in mischief at school. Tall, auburn-haired, full of confidence and merriment. Some of Harry's spirit had faded during her marriage but Eleanor had been happy to see the spark returning to her dark eyes. She'd drawn Eleanor and Mary in with her, despite their sadness and worry.

'I have the most fascinating plan to fill my time and I need your help...'

The plan turned out to be the St Aubin and Briggs Confidential Agency. Harry said she never wanted anyone caught in a marriage like hers if she could help it. She'd successfully paired up several of her friends at her marital home at Briggs Manor and her reputation had spread until people she barely even knew sought her out for assistance.

'My income is not as plump as one might wish,' Harry had declared. *'And how can I resist doing my tiny bit to bring some happiness into the world!'*

And so their business had been born and it had flourished. An office and lodgings in Kingston Buildings, right across from the Abbey and within walking distance of everyplace important. Pretty clothes for pretty Mary. Lots of books for Eleanor. Luscious Bath buns galore for Miss Muffins, who lived up to her name. They were all together, not to be parted despite the lack of any fine fortunes or grand connections. And Harry was proved right—the work was deeply satisfying, every new couple's blissful smiles a few drops of sunshine in a grey world.

The agency did nothing so vulgar as advertise, of course, or put out signs on their doors. They were strictly by referral. Past patrons giving letters of recommendation to those in need. Whispers at the Pump Room or the Theatre Royal to a friend who might need a tiny push in the right direction. Bath was filled with those seeking their perfect partner. It was as if being amid illness and uncertainty made people long for more from life.

Yes, it was fine work, and Eleanor enjoyed it. She'd long known that she herself would never marry. She had to look after Mary, be like a mother to her and make sure their family was safe. That was her task. Having work she enjoyed was a great comfort. But sometimes there was a potential patron who was just a bit—extra.

She made sure her expression remained serene, politely interested, *not* giggling and turned back to Mr Higgleston-Worth. He had been sent to them by Lord Kembleton, a gentleman the agency matched with a very pretty young widow several months ago, one of their first successes. So of course they wanted to help any friend of Lord and Lady Kembleton, though it was hard to imagine Mr Higgleston-Worth knowing such an amiable pair. Lord Kembleton was portly, amiable and quick to laugh. His new wife was sweet and funny.

Mr H-W was none of those things. He minced and chattered and demanded, constantly smoothing the few strands of his hair still clinging to his scalp and oiled flat, the copious gold buttons on his red and blue plaid waistcoat threatening to burst with every word. He purported to having retired from the Army as a wealthy man, but Eleanor had some trouble picturing him in a warrior light.

An image suddenly flashed into her mind, quite unbidden. Fred Canning in his fine red coat, as she last saw him, his golden hair shining in the faint glow of the summerhouse. The warm press of his kiss to her hand, the way he smiled at her. How often she'd thought of him in the years since then! *Too* often. As she went over the agency ledgers, or paid tradesmens' bills, thoughts of him would pop randomly into her head. His laugh, his lemon and sunshine scent and the touch of his hand on hers. The fleeting joy of his kiss on her hand. The deep, warm chocolate sound of his voice as he read poetry to her in their secret summerhouse place. It was maddening.

She'd heard wisps of information about him over the years, of course, when they still lived at the vicarage. The whole neighbourhood was shocked to hear of his wounding at Waterloo. They'd hoped he might come back to Moulton Magna when his mother died, but he did not. She did not see him again.

After Eleanor left for Bath, Fred's father and then his older brother died in quick, tragic succession and everyone knew he *must* return then. He was the Earl now! And Eleanor heard via letters from old friends in the neighbourhood the most shocking thing of all. Fred had become a notorious rake in his years in the Army. She knew then he had only and ever considered her a friend. She had not believed such rumours at first, not of the man who had been her friend. She'd clung to the memory of what they once had, until she realised from reading tales of battles how such things could change a person. She'd been forced to think it must be true, to put Fred out of her mind. She'd been so silly to ever think there could be anything between them besides friendship, neighbours!

Yet still she grieved for the man she thought she knew.

'Two thousand pounds a year! Surely I deserve the very best,' Mr Higgleston-Worth cried emphatically, pulling Eleanor back from her memories.

She blinked hard and focused on Mr H-W. It was not at all like her to be distracted when she was meant to be working. Patrons deserved all her attention, even ones as ridiculous as Mr H-W.

'Indeed, Mr Higgleston-Worth,' she said soothingly and glanced down at the papers on her desk.

Everything they asked potential patrons about their family—places of residence, age and appearance, income, wishes and hopes in a spouse—was asked about most delicately, of course. The ladies always desired a secure home, a guaranteed jointure for their future and someone kind. The gentlemen desired someone pretty and of sweet nature, adept at running a household. Mr Higgleston-Worth's list of wishes was perhaps a bit more, er, elaborate.

'A lady with a fine dowry. Good teeth. Shiny hair.

Preferably blonde, but a very light brown would be acceptable. No novel readers, they are too frivolous. A fashionable dresser, but not extravagant. Small feet. Not a loud laugher.'

Eleanor studied him again. Two thousand a year was nothing to sneeze at. Some of their patrons lived on far less and still found romance. But it was not the amount of grandiose riches a man like Mr H-W would really need to attract 'the best'. This was a challenge indeed.

Luckily, this was just a first meeting. No contracts had been agreed upon yet.

'I have much to offer,' Mr Higgleston-Worth said again, tapping at those shining buttons. 'And I would thus insist on the finest qualities in a lady. I must be wed by the end of the year.'

Eleanor considered this. It was late summer now. Not much time at all, especially for such a vast undertaking. Usually the arrangements for the agency's months were most careful and deliberate. Several interviews, references, things of that nature. It was a most personal business. But a business, nonetheless. Their reputation rested on making harmonious, durable matches.

'Thank you, Mr Higgleston-Worth,' she said. 'We shall be in contact very soon.'

Mr H-W spluttered. 'What do you mean, be in contact? I expected a match *now*!' He waved a pudgy, beringed hand at the rows of file cabinets lining the blue-papered wall behind the desk. 'Find one in there! I have two thousand a year.'

Eleanor heard Mary gasp. She feared her sister would burst into laughter, which in turn would make her laugh.

'Our process is very careful, Mr Higgleston-Worth. I am sure you must appreciate that as an organised military gentleman. We want all our patrons to have every success on this vital endeavour and that requires the closest consideration.'

She rang the bell that sat before her, three times—an urgent summons. Daisy, their maid, appeared at once. 'Daisy shall see you out and I assure you, we will write as soon as possible.'

Daisy, very well-trained in her job and practised in the ways of the agency, ushered a spluttering Mr Higgleston-Worth out. The door slid shut behind him to a merciful silence.

Until Mary burst into peals of laughter and Eleanor couldn't help but join her. Miss Muffins barked and twirled.

'Oh, heavens!' Mary gasped, wiping at her eyes, her upswept blonde curls trembling. 'I don't think we have seen quite such a specimen since—since…'

'Perhaps Mr Morris? That man who came here at Christmas, who claimed to be a widower of forty…'

'And was seventy if he was a day. But at least he had better taste in waistcoats.'

'Yes. And we did find a wife for him, remember? Lady Henderson. She was a most sensible and forthright lady, who would not put up with any nonsense. And we were handsomely rewarded. Surely, with two thousand a year, Mr Higgleston-Worth could equal that? With a lady of strong will?'

Eleanor frowned as she studied their precious file cabinets, going through those papers in her mind. There were a few ladies who had lingered there a bit longer than she would like, who were a challenge to match for one reason or another. Perhaps one of them might suit Mr H-W? Did they have a blind lady, mayhap?

'Mrs Miller? Or perhaps Lady Hayes? Or her companion! She was a pretty young lady, if terribly shy. Though who could blame her with Lady Hayes as her employer,' Eleanor murmured.

'Hmm, yes! Miss—Perkins, was it? I would love to see her escape such employment.' Mary rose in a flurry of pale blue striped skirts and hurried to open one of the upper drawers, sorting through the array of carefully curated files. 'Oh, there must be someone in here…'

Eleanor drifted towards the window, Miss Muffins at her heels. She stretched her aching shoulders after a long morning of interviews.

She glimpsed a man striding across the square between Kingston Buildings and the Abbey, taller than most in the crowds around him, and supremely eye-catching, even in a plain, dark blue greatcoat. His wide-brimmed hat concealed most of his face, except a square, adorably dimpled jaw and surprisingly full, sensual lips. He was slim-hipped, broad-shouldered and moved with an easy, loose, loping grace. He made Eleanor think of a most extraordinary acrobat they had recently seen with a travelling circus and she tracked his progress with fascination, much like all the ladies he passed.

'I shall go fetch some buns from Sally Lunn's for our tea, Mary,' she said, suddenly feeling restless, and took her dark green pelisse and plain straw bonnet from their hooks. She glanced in the small looking glass to make sure her bonnet ribbons were straight, her dark curls still tidy in their plain coil. She would never be as pretty as doll-like, golden Mary, or tall, Greek goddess Harry, but she could be presentable enough. Not that she had such hopes for herself any longer. She had given that up long ago and now hoped only to help others find their romantic dreams. It had to be enough.

And she wasn't going out just for another look at the man in the wide-brimmed hat. She was *not*.

'Hmm,' Mary answered, buried in a stack of files. Once Mary became determined to find a challenging match, there was no stopping her. She looked delicate and sweet, but she was relentless. 'And some strawberry jam? I think it was all gone at breakfast.'

'Of course. I'll post these letters, as well.' As she gathered up the missives, Miss Muffins peeked from beneath the desk where she had retreated again with a hopeful tail-wag. She had been a rescue pup, found by Eleanor and Harry cowering half-starved under a bridge. She was usually an angel of manners, but she *did* love a good run. And a fine Sally Lunn's bun. 'Very well, Miss Muffins. You may come, too.'

She found Miss Muffins' lead and the two of them made their way down the stairs, past the elegant leaf-green and gold drawing room where patrons sometimes waited and took tea and out through the black-painted front door. It was a typical Bath day. Grey-skied, threatening rain, clouds scudding past overhead. Eleanor blinked at the sudden grey glare after the house, spots in front of her eyes, but Miss Muffins was in a great hurry. She ran to the end of the lead and yanked hard, catching Eleanor off-guard.

'Here, let me help you, madame,' a voice said. A most familiar voice. The voice that had so long haunted her daydreams. Surely this could not be real?

Eleanor blinked up and saw a dark shadow—the man she'd glimpsed from the window earlier. How could Fred's voice come from that gentleman? Had she conjured it from her wistful earlier, her memories? She felt so very slow and silly for a moment. As if she waded through molasses, through dreams, caught between *now* and *then*. Even Miss Muffins was silent with confusion and wonder.

He knelt beside her, his gloved hands reaching for the scattered letters. He even *felt* handsome, the sort of man a woman just wanted to stare and stare at and get lost in. There was such a quiet confidence about him. She dared to peek up at him, hoping it might actually be Fred even as she feared to see him again. Feared for him to see what she had become, a plain, quiet little spinster.

That hat, unfashionably wide-brimmed, hid most of his face as he looked down at his task, but she was sure it *was* Fred. That dimple, incongruously adorable above the hard, sharp line of his chiselled jaw. Those lips, even though they were bracketed with harsh new lines, were surely the same that had once kissed her hand so warmly, so lingeringly.

'Fred,' she whispered.

He suddenly went very still. Frozen like one of the carvings on the Abbey that rose above them. For one long, endless, taut moment she thought he might flee from her. He seemed quite as startled as she, but not in a good surprise way. Not in a *here is my old dear friend* way. In a *must flee...trapped* way.

Had she done something, said something wrong? She felt suddenly bereft, cold even in that warm day. Yet how could that be? They hadn't met in years. But now, so close to him again, she felt he'd only been away for a moment. That no time had passed between them at all.

He did not seem to feel the same. He was so very still, his head bent down. Slowly, ever so slowly, he turned to face her and her breath became trapped in her lungs. Those eyes, Fred's sky-blue eyes, glittered from the shadows under his hat. Every spark of that old humour, that old light-heartedness, had vanished from their depths. Even when she had tried to forget Fred, she'd sometimes dared to imagine how it might be to see him again. This did not seem like the man of her imaginings at all. He seemed a stranger.

'Eleanor,' he said at last, the word toneless. Distant. He stood and held out her letters and she scrambled to her feet. 'It's been quite some time.'

'Indeed. Many years. Yes,' she stammered, try-ing not to recall how she remembered every one of those years, every month. She hated how breathless and squeaking her voice sounded, when she wanted to be sophisticated, breezy, careless. Not like she longed to jump up and embrace him, hold him close. 'I—we heard you left the Army. After Waterloo. After—well, I heard you were wounded and then...' And then he raced and wenched through London, according to the gossip. Moved into a world so far from her own.

He still seemed so wary. 'Yes, I did leave the Army after Waterloo. I've been visiting my stepmother here in Bath.' He paused, glancing away as if he sought an escape. 'I was sorry to hear about your father. He was a good man.'

'Thank you. Yes, indeed he was.' Even though he ended her dreams of school and an independent life, needed her so very much to keep his house and nurse him. She'd loved him and thinking of him made her shiver. She started to tell him that she, too, was sorry for the loss of his parents and brother. But he seemed to silence any words like that. Didn't want to hear them.

'And this is where you have lived since his death? In Bath?' he asked quietly.

'Yes. My father's curate was granted the living and Mary and I had to leave…' She did not mention that the curate, Mr Neville, had made noises about wanting to marry her and make her the vicarage's permanent housekeeper, but she could not do that. 'Our friend Lady Briggs offered us a home here.'

'And what do you do here? Do you like it in Bath?'

'Oh, yes, it's a lovely place to live and I do…' She gestured helplessly, not knowing how to explain her strange occupation. She had given up hopes for a loving marriage for herself a long time ago, as long ago as the last time she saw Fred. She had to take care of Mary, be the head of their little family. Now she just wanted to help others who might be as lonely as she had once been. As she still was so often. He brought old dreams back too sharply, too painfully. 'I do things.'

A smile finally quirked at the corner of his lips. 'Things?'

Miss Muffins whined a bit, gazing adoringly up at Fred. Just like all the ladies he'd walked past.

Fred knelt down to pat her head, sending her into tail-wagging ecstasies. 'She's a pretty pup,' he said, his voice filled with an easy gentleness that reminded her of the old Fred. Not the distant new stranger. 'I only knew hunting hounds growing up, but my stepmother has a pug. I thought it a silly little, squishy thing at first, but...' He rubbed Miss Muffins' head, his smile widening. 'They are very good company. They ask no questions, have no expectations.'

Eleanor wondered with a pang if that was a hint. If he thought she had 'expectations'.

'Indeed, they are very dear. Mary and I quite dote on Miss Muffins. She...'

A sudden gust of wind caught at Fred's hat and sent it sailing from his head, barely caught in his fist before it escaped entirely. Eleanor couldn't quite catch her own shocked gasp before it left her lips. Half of Fred's face, once so unworldly and handsome, was scarred, puckered and pink. She felt appalled that he could have felt any pain, longed to make it all better somehow, some way.

'Oh, Fred...' she whispered.

'The war,' he snapped shortly and thrust the letters into her hand.

She reached for his face, the dear face she'd dreamed

of for so long, her heart aching for what he must have suffered. For the fact that she hadn't been there for him. But he flinched and her hand dropped away. 'Is it—painful?' she whispered.

His scowl faded and he seemed to soften a bit, swaying towards her. 'Not any longer. I barely think of it.'

Yet he hid it behind his hat, behind his fast, brusque movements. Beyond his eyes, that no longer sparkled with laughter.

Eleanor swallowed hard and glanced away. 'Lady Fleetwood lives here now?' she asked, reaching for any change of topic. She didn't want him to go yet. Didn't want to lose him again quite so soon. 'We only met her a few times before we left the neighbourhood, but she seemed very kind.'

'Indeed, she is. She has been a good friend to me. She was ill for a time after my father died, but the waters seem to have done her much good. She looks forward to mixing more in Bath society now.'

'And you? Are you looking forward to social occasions?' To finding a wife, maybe? She hated the pang such a thought gave her. But perhaps that really was what brought him back after all this time. To marry, start a family, be the Earl he must be. 'We are not London but there is the theatre, the assemblies, the subscription concerts...'

His expression snapped closed again, a shutter going down between them. 'I have a great deal of business to see to before I return to Moulton Magna.'

'Yes. Of course,' she whispered, embarrassed as she recalled the gossip about the current bankrupt state of the estate, thanks to the late earl's secret debts. That would all be on Fred's shoulders now. No matter he looked so much harder, so much older. No wonder everything in her longed to reach for him, comfort him. The one thing she could not do.

As if he could read her thoughts, as if he, too, yearned for some of their old connection, he suddenly reached out and softly, warmly, achingly touched her hand. 'It is so nice to see you again, Ella. You look— you look very well indeed.'

Ella. His old name for her. She smiled back and slid her hand away before she could seize him right there in the middle of the street, wrap her arms around him and never let him go.

'It must be the waters,' she made herself say with a light laugh. 'They say they are miracle workers! Do bring Lady Fleetwood to call on us soon. We should so much like to see her again. She was very kind when we had to leave the vicarage so quickly.'

'I shall. She would like to see you again, too.' Those terrible shutters came down again, hiding his thoughts and feelings from her. He bowed so politely, so correctly. 'Good day.'

She curtsied in return. 'Good day.'

She forced herself to turn away, to not look back even though everything in her longed to do just that. It was the most difficult thing she'd ever done, turning her back on him and walking away as if nothing had changed, nothing was wrong. That her heart did not ache. Even Miss Muffins dragged at her lead, reluctant to leave him.

'Did you fetch the buns for tea already?' Mary called as Eleanor stood frozen in the corridor, Miss Muffins watching her in puzzlement that they hadn't finished the promised walk. That they left her new friend behind. 'You must have run like Atalanta!'

Eleanor glanced down at the letters still in her hand and laughed wryly to realise she had entirely forgotten any errands at all. Forgotten everything about Fred and the golden glow of the past. 'Oh, Mary dearest. You will never guess who has come to Bath…'

Chapter Three

'Marriage would do you such good, Fred,' Penelope, his stepmama—though it still felt wrong to call her that, as she was only ten years his senior and looked ten years his junior—said with a wistful sigh. Pen filled a rose-painted teacup and handed it to him over the table, giving him that worried little smile he'd come to dread.

'It would *not*, believe me Pen,' he said. He took a sip of the tea and wished it contained something a wee bit stronger. It might help him get through this perpetual-seeming conversation. 'I do like my life as it is. Quiet and peaceful at last. And who would have me, as I am now?' He gestured towards his scars, his twisted left hand. 'No amount of visits to the baths can fix this you know.'

Penelope laughed, her brown eyes glowing. Fred's gruff old father really had been the most fortunate and undeserving of men to win her hand. She was so pretty. Petite and dark-haired, so kind and laughing. She had been a dear friend to him when he came home, wounded and wild as a bear. She deserved much better than what she had, a few years with a grumpy, debt-ridden man in a crumbling estate and now this tiny house in Sunderland Street on a small jointure. He longed to give her more. To repay some of the friendship she'd shown him when he so needed it. For nursing him when he returned home so damaged and angry, withdrawing from society and fed up with all people in general.

Fed up with all people—except Eleanor St Aubin. He could scarcely believe his vision when she appeared so suddenly before him again! Ella, whose memory had so long sustained him on so many endless, pain-filled dark nights. Her smile, the music of her laughter, the wild curl of her autumn-brown hair, the dreamy look in her eyes when she read to him from *The Fairy Queen* and talked of adventures.

He'd thought never to see her again, when he heard through Penelope's letters that Eleanor's father had died and she and her sister left the neighbourhood. The idea of her being lost for ever had pained him almost more than the scars on his cheek. To never hear her dreams again, never watch her dashing through the sunlight, always just beyond his reach. Her sweetness and innocence, things he'd thought vanished in the mud and blood of war. He'd had a wild notion to find her again once he returned to Moulton Magna and took up the title, then cold reality set in, as it always did now. He couldn't bear for her to see him this way, the way he had become. Couldn't bear to see revulsion and embarrassment in her eyes, as he saw in so many.

Then—there she was. In an instant, on that street here in Bath, like a dream bursting into bright reality.

It had been another long, dark-shadowed night, filled with nightmare visions of explosions, fire, death and pain. Friends blown to bits, the ground caving beneath him. At first, he thought he was still dreaming when he saw her, tempting visions of hope and light born of sheer exhaustion.

Once, she'd been his friend. His Fairy Queen. His haven of laughter and easy acceptance of life in a place where he never felt he belonged. A home that was empty and silent. He'd always wanted to be truly worthy of her approval, worthy of her goodness, even though he'd known that was impossible. Especially once he went to London and discovered the temptations there…

It was now even more impossible. As far away as the moon. If only he'd been given warning that she was near, so he could hide! So she wouldn't see him that way, so different from what he once was.

Yet, selfishly, he was glad he'd met with her. Seen her, touched her hand, smelled her floral summertime perfume. Known she was real again, that she truly was standing in front of him.

Like him, she was older than in his golden memories. The girl at Moulton Magna was a woman now. A beautiful woman, delicate and slender, with shining dark hair and sweet, sad eyes. What happened to her since last they met? The loss of her father and home, surely, but what he saw in those eyes was more than that. It was as if she was older than her years now, as he was, as if she had seen much. He longed to know everything, to ask her every detail of every lost minute. Just to hear her voice, sit in the peace and light that always seemed to surround her.

But he couldn't ask her to stay with *him* and what he was now. A scarred man who had done terrible things in the name of battle. A man with a house and estate falling down around him that was his responsibility to save now.

The silence in the drawing room had grown long and he was suddenly jolted by the awareness that Penelope watched him carefully, waiting for him to speak, to do *something.* She was always patient, always watchful, just like Ella.

And she saw too much.

He smiled at her and held his cup out for more tea, even if there was no whisky to go with it. 'Sorry, Pen. I'm no good at being an earl out in society yet.'

She refilled his cup and added more salmon sandwiches to his plate before slipping one of them to her puppy. She was quite sure Fred didn't eat enough, didn't look after himself and perhaps she was right. There were so many other things to do now, so much to worry him.

'Just one more reason you need a wife,' Penelope said. 'Someone to run your household properly, help you with your work, accept invitations. You cannot do it alone. And then there is—well, there is the money…'

Fred grimaced, remembering how extravagant Moulton Magna seemed in his childhood—always parties and hunts and new art and jewels around his mother's neck. All paid for with imaginary coin, it seemed. But the house and the family had been the centre of the neighbourhood, relied on by so many people.

'I cannot say you are entirely wrong, Pen. But there is a distant cousin somewhere, if I can't come up to scratch.' Not that the cousin wanted the blasted title any more than Fred did.

Penelope shook her head. 'He's not at all suited to the title.'

Fred gave a harsh bark of laughter. 'And I am?'

'You give yourself far too little credit. You are intelligent and resourceful. You care about the people on the estate. They need you!'

'You are not wrong about that,' he admitted, feeling supremely grumpy about it all. This was never meant to be his job. He hadn't been trained for it and now he was damaged in the bargain. The people of the estate deserved better. 'I do have duties now, as terrible as I may be at them. And a countess would be a useful thing. But as I said, Pen, who would have me? Looking like this, with no money, a shambles of a house...' He laughed, but there was shame there, too. Shame that he, who had been a fine soldier, couldn't solve this problem.

Penelope winced, as they both remembered that the once grand Moulton Magna, a showpiece of elegance and culture, had started to fall down around them. Leaking roofs, fading furniture, bare patches on the mouldy walls where paintings once hung.

'It would be a challenge to be mistress of Moulton Magna, that's true. I certainly found it to be so. But you would be a better husband than your father could ever have been. You would be a true partner to the right lady, a lady of taste and breeding. You used to be handsome as a god, Fred, and you are still a fine-looking man! Three-quarters of perfection is still quite blasted perfect, you know.'

He laughed in surprise. '*Blasted*, Pen?'

Her cheeks turned bright pink and she laughed, too. 'I am a widow, I'm allowed to curse sometimes. And you *do* give yourself too little credit. You are young and energetic and spirited now that you are regaining your health. A hero of the battlefield! Moulton Magna is not at its best right now, perhaps, yet it is an ancient estate with much history and beautiful grounds and being a countess is no small prize. Ladies of…'

'Ladies of fortune?' he said.

Penelope blushed again and turned away to feed her dog another sandwich. 'I suppose she would have to be, yes.'

'Taste, breeding *and* money. Where shall we have to find such a paragon?' He thought again of Ella. Always of Ella and her bursting, bright smile when she saw him again. Her hand warm through her glove.

'Bath is full of ladies seeking marriage, you know.'

'Do you have any suggestions? Particular candidates in mind?'

She fussed with the tea tray, rearranging the silver pot and the cups. 'I do not have a certain lady in mind, no. I am too solitary these days to know all the gossip, I fear. But I do know someone who could help.'

Fred thought her determined expression, like an officer planning a campaign, was terrifying. Yet he sensed there was no escape. What other solution could there be? Where could he turn? Other men married for advantage all the time, he knew that well, but he'd never thought to be one. 'Who might that be?'

She glanced up with a new, eager smile. 'I was talking to an old friend of my mother's last week, a Lady Hemston...'

Fred shook his head hard, horrified. 'I know her! I couldn't marry someone she would choose. Have you seen her army of nieces?'

Penelope laughed. She suddenly looked so young, as she had before her marriage. Young as Ella once had, as he had, before life turned all of them upside down. 'Oh, heavens, no! But one of those nieces was recently betrothed to a marquess. Everyone was quite sure she would never wed at all but she and her fiancé are utterly wild about each other! Lady Hemston told me, in the strictest of confidence so you must not breathe a word, that they had a bit of—assistance in the engagement endeavour.'

Fred was now even more worried. 'Assistance?'

'Yes. An agency of sorts, most discreet, with an excellent reputation. They are only to be found by referral, though I am sure word of their fine work has spread through Bath and beyond by now.'

'Agency?' That sounded ominous.

'Oh, Fred, do stop saying words in that way! It is an unusual organisation, yes, but we are in an unusual situation and we could use their help. *You* need their help.'

'Is this a brothel of some sort, Pen? Because I assure you, despite my injuries, those things are quite, er, in working order.'

'Frederick!' she cried. '*No*. This is a *marital* agency. They help people find their perfect match. Their *respectable* match. When the usual channels of finding a spouse do not quite work as they should.'

He laughed at the idea of someone marching around Bath pairing people up. 'Matchmaking, is it?'

'Yes. They are quite good at it and as I said they are very discreet. Discerning. We could at least consult them. Ask their advice?'

'And have our family business known all over Bath in a day.'

Penelope sighed in exasperation. 'Fred. Everyone already knows our business. But these ladies are hardly strangers. They are known as the St Aubin and Briggs Confidential Agency and two of them are the St Aubin sisters. Daughters of our old vicar, perfectly respectable and commendable. Perhaps you remember them?'

'Eleanor St Aubin?' he whispered. The memory of her eyes flashed through his mind, her smile, her sombre dark green pelisse and plain bonnet. His Fairy Queen. A matchmaker? 'She is the one who runs this—agency?'

'Yes, Eleanor! Such a dear lady, they were so good to me when I married your papa. I was sorry to see them leave the neighbourhood so suddenly. And there is her younger sister Miss Mary, along with Lady Briggs. I saw the Misses St Aubin at the Pump Room a few weeks ago, after I first arrived, but was not able to say hello to them then. I have been thinking I should call on them, now that my mourning is officially over. If they *could* be of assistance…'

Fred closed his eyes against a headache building inside of him like a vice at the thought of Ella of all people knowing *all* his business. Scanning the ladies of Bath to find him a wife. Ella thinking less of him than she probably already did. 'I should not like to put Miss St Aubin to such trouble. To presume on our acquaintance…'

Penelope gave a puzzled frown. 'But surely old friends would not mind! They would be happy to help. Everyone at Moulton Magna always spoke so highly of the St Aubin girls and Lady Briggs is such a leader of society here in Bath.'

'I saw Eleanor today, near the Abbey,' he blurted.

Her eyes widened. 'Did you? And she remembered you? Even better!'

'Pen…' he said. 'I don't want them to—that is…' He couldn't let an old friend assist him in such an embarrassing endeavour. Especially not one who had been his best friend once. Who he would wish could be more than that now.

She leaned forward and gently touched his wrist, just above his damaged hand. 'I say again, my dear Fred, you need a wife. If old friends, people who know you well, can be of assistance, I'm happy to ask them for their advice. Did you not like the St Aubins in some way, when you lived near them?'

Fred had another image of Eleanor running through a summer meadow, her curling hair flying behind her,

her laughter on the breeze. The sheer life and sweetness of her. 'Yes. I liked them very much.'

Penelope sat back, a speculative gleam coming into her eyes. 'Then let me call on them. I should do so anyway, as an old neighbour. I can see what their thoughts might be on our delicate subject.'

Fred pushed himself to his feet and strode to the window, feeling the surge of some of his old energy moving through his veins. As if just remembering Eleanor, talking of her, brought his old self back again. His old hopes and dreams.

'Very well,' he said at last and heard Penelope clap her hands in approval. At least he could make Pen happy for a while, and also have an excuse to see Ella again. To talk to her, see her smile, just for a little longer. 'We will call on them. But I do not want their help in finding a wife. Not at all.'

Chapter Four

'In short, Lady Briggs, Miss St Aubin—I fear if you do not help my poor, dear daughter, she will be quite lost! Entirely on the shelf. Alone in this cold and dreadful world. *Desolate* of all consolation!'

As Mrs Evans's voice climbed higher and higher, like a soprano straining mightily for a dramatic finale at the Theatre Royal, Eleanor stared hard at the notebook open in front of her and blinked. She feared if she looked at Harry she would giggle, which would then make Harry guffaw—Harry loved any opportunity to laugh—and then it would all be over. The Evans family would be lost as patrons, which would be too bad as Mr Evans had in recent years found rich seams of coal on his lands, and had a mercantile empire on top it all. Thanks heavens Mary wasn't there to giggle, too! She had gone to take Miss Muffins for a walk, luckily.

If the agency could help Miss Evans out of 'lonely desolation,' the greengrocers and the butchers would have their bills paid for some time to come and that could only be most desirable.

As Mrs Evans dabbed at her eyes with a lacy handkerchief and went on with her laments, Eleanor discreetly studied Miss Evans, and thought the girl did have much potential. She had a lovely, peachy complexion and large hazel eyes, honey-coloured hair peeking from beneath her flower-bedecked bonnet.

She'd said only about three words since they arrived, but who could blame her? No one could get a single syllable out with Mrs Evans there. But once Miss Evans learned to make the very most of herself, to speak up, and with such a nice dowry in the offering, she should have no worries in the marriage mart.

The challenge would be getting her away from her mother and finding out what *she* wanted. That would help her find the *right* sort of gentleman. Someone to make her happy, not just some fortune hunter.

Eleanor sighed. A challenge indeed, but they'd seen far worse at the agency.

'Will need a better dancing master, of course!' Mrs Evans was saying. 'And a new coiffure. Who does the Duchess of Raine's hair? We saw her at the opera last week, so charming. That hairdresser might do. If my girl would only smile more! Engage the young men with a bit of bright chatter, a smile or two. I've told her and told her…'

Miss Evans stared hard out of the window, her lips pinched together in way that would never 'engage the young men', but Eleanor couldn't blame her.

'I think Miss Evans should have no trouble at all in finding a suitable, indeed a very happy, match,' Harry said soothingly. She was so good at that, at appearing always confident and assuring no matter who the patron might be. Her elegant morning gown of purple striped silk and fine pearl earrings didn't hurt. If she could achieve such things, she could help anyone else do it, too!

Mrs, Evans frowned doubtfully. 'Are you certain, Lady Briggs?'

'Of course. A lovely young lady from such a good family? No trouble at all. It would have to be just the *right* sort of person, of course. One must be so careful.' Harry turned a page in her own notebook. 'Tell me, Miss Evans—what do you envisage in your future husband?'

Miss Evans glanced uncertainly at her mother.

'A vicar, perhaps?' Eleanor said, thinking of her own good-natured papa. 'Or a man with a small country estate, well known to all his neighbours.' A quiet young lady might well enjoy a familiar environment with a kindly squire.

'Oh, no! Our daughter can surely aim higher than that,' Mrs Evans cried.

It was rather a relief when they departed half an hour later, all their information entered in the agency books to be reviewed later. As their footsteps faded down the stairs and Daisy shut the door behind them, Harry collapsed onto the settee with a deep sigh and kicked up her purple satin slippers.

'Goodness me,' she said. 'I always longed for a mama, growing up with only my father after my poor mother died birthing me, but patrons such as Mrs Evans make me wonder if I was quite wrong in those dreams of motherly love and support.'

Eleanor laughed ruefully and flipped through her pages of new notes. 'Mary and I were certainly fortunate in our darling mother and I miss her vastly. But I can't help but think she might have been quite as anxious about the marriage mart as Mrs Evans, with two daughters to secure. Not that she would have gone about it this way...'

'Worrying is not really something Miss Evans needs to think about, with a bit of guidance. Though she must be extra wary of men seeking only fortune. Her dowry is truly a stupendous one. Really, all the Evans need to do is march her around the Pump Room after having our dear Master of Ceremonies spread a quiet word or two. And finding a better modiste, of course. That pelisse! But I suspect that was Mrs Evans' doing.' She laid back against the cushions and stared up at the ceiling as if envisaging a line of eligible young men. 'I'm glad they brought her here, though. No one deserves such a fate as being married for one's fortune. Especially not a girl who seems as shy as Miss Evans.'

A shadow seemed to drift over Harry's beautiful face, perhaps memories of her own unhappy marriage to a man much older than herself and Eleanor started to go to her. But then Harry just laughed and turned away, hiding her thoughts again.

'Perhaps we could winkle her away from her mother under the guise of a dance lesson or two,' Eleanor suggested. She took out another ledger—the account of all the people they employed when assistance was needed. Dance masters, music teachers, etiquette experts and modistes. One of them could surely be brought to the office and teach Miss Evans, along with some young men, the latest steps.

'What about that sweet Mr Monroe we met last week? Or Lord Perry? He is a shy young man himself. He'd be sure to be patient and kind with a lady like Miss Evans. His estate is nothing compared to Mr Evans, of course, but his house is very pretty indeed and in a quiet part of the country. And he has a respectable income and no wastrel habits.'

'Oh, what a good thought, Eleanor dear! Lord Perry is a darling boy. It's too bad about the shyness. It would be so nice to see him and Miss Evans ride off together to private country bliss.'

Eleanor laughed. It was her very favourite part of their work, when a thought, a fragment of an instinct, could lead to a happy lifetime for two people.

She only wondered, hoped…

She shook her head hard. Even beginning to wish for such a spark for herself was silly and futile. Her future had been decided long ago, when she was deemed the sensible one, the one who would look after her family. She had to take the bits of happiness from the people she worked for and warm herself in the glow of their happiness.

It had been enough, more than she could have expected in the days of her vicarage drudgery, that she might live in a fine town and meet so many interesting people. Help them in some way. She loved her work. The satisfaction of it and the life she and Mary and Harry had built there.

What was wrong with her today? She'd been terri-

bly distracted! She needed to focus on the challenge at
hand, yet her gaze kept drifting out through the window to the cathedral across the way and the crowds
passing below. Her thoughts very far away from their
ledgers and patrons.

It was the return of Fred. She was sure of it. Seeing
him again after so very long. How changed he was!
And yet his eyes, those wonderful sky-blue eyes, were
almost the same. Her Redcrosse Knight.

'Do you think, Eleanor?' Harry asked.

Eleanor blinked, jerked back from her sky-floating
daydreams into the daily routine of their office. 'I'm
sorry, Harry, I was wool-gathering.'

Harry tilted her head, a puzzled little frown on her
lips. 'I was just saying perhaps we could take Miss
Evans to the theatre. Introduce her to Lord Perry there.
Without Mrs Evans.'

'A fine idea. I hear they are doing *School for Scandal* next week,' Eleanor said vaguely, her gaze drifting
back to the window.

'Are you quite sure you're well today? It isn't like
you to be distracted and you do look a little pale. Should
I have Daisy bring up a bottle of claret with the tea tray?
The doctors do say it strengthens the blood.'

Eleanor smiled at her, hoping it looked reassuring.
'I wouldn't say no to a wee drop. I am just a bit tired.
I didn't sleep well last night. I don't mean to be dis-
tracted with our patrons.'

'Of course you aren't! You never could be. You're
always the soul of kindness and understanding. They
love you. You are the backbone to this whole enter-

prise.' Harry lifted Miss Muffins onto the settee with her, still watching Eleanor carefully. 'Is there some reason you've been sleepless lately, my dear?'

Eleanor stared down at the desk, fiddling with the papers to keep from looking right at Harry. Her friend had always been so perceptive. It was a great strength in business but a nuisance when one had a secret. 'I just—well, I saw an old friend again, that's all. Someone I haven't met with since we lived at the vicarage. It's brought back such memories.'

'Ahh…' Harry nodded sagely. 'A man from your past.'

Eleanor laughed uncertainly, shuffling more papers. She only served to put them in disarray. 'Yes, he was one of the sons of our neighbour. And now he is an earl. He went into the Army and was wounded at Waterloo. It has—he has changed greatly. As he would have done, of course. But the change seemed like it wasn't just—not just physical.' Surely dreadful things had happened to him in battle. Things she ached to consider.

Harry's smile turned soft, sympathetic. 'You had feelings for this earl?'

Eleanor shook her head. 'Maybe once. Just a schoolgirl thing. He was so very handsome. Such fun. And he treated me like a person and not just a silly girl. We read together, *The Fairy Queen*, explored the estate and talked. Talked about so very many things.'

'And what was it like to see him again?'

Astounding. Wonderful. Terrible. 'Unnerving, I would say.'

Harry leaned forward, her expression solemn and

intent. 'Eleanor. You are so very good at our work. So caring with the patrons and careful of their happiness. Careful of everyone.'

'I do try, Harry. How else are we to pay for our soup and wine?'

'No, it's more than that. Mary and I like the agency, of course. We like the people and the romance of it all. But for you, I think it runs deeper. As if you wish you could make all the world happy.'

And that was impossible. She couldn't even make Fred happy, not now. 'It's the vicar's daughter in me, I suppose. I do want everyone to be comfortable and content.'

'And our files are filled with grateful letters attesting to your success! But what about *you*?'

'Me?'

'Wouldn't you like a match for *you*?'

Eleanor was shocked. 'I—I hadn't thought of such a thing. No. No, I am happy with the spinster life. Aren't you?' Once she'd been happy with such a life or at least resigned to it. She'd never met a man who made her feel as Fred once did and a marriage of convenience held no attraction for her. She had to look after Mary, run their business. But now—now maybe that life didn't seem quite so content as it once did.

'Certainly I am. Our work. The independence of it and not answering to anyone else at all. It's my dream come true after that nightmare with old Briggs. I have no desire to wed again.'

'Yet you think I would?'

'It would be different for you.'

'How so?'

Harry smiled sadly. 'I was just a girl when I married. I knew nothing of the world and had no choice in the matter. My parents arranged it all. They needed the money so much. You and I—we know how to make suitable matches, happy matches. It's our work, after all. We can see what makes two people compatible. What sort of lives they wish to lead together.'

'Our instincts do seem correct more often than not,' Eleanor said, thinking of the careful formulas they applied to their matches and the musing over personalities, wishes and wants. Yet none of that explained her feelings for Fred—the past, present and dreams all mixed up in a jumble.

'Perhaps we should try our instincts on you! I did hate being married but you would not, I'm sure. Not with the right person. You should have a comfortable home, companionship and fun.'

Once, she'd hoped for all those same things. She'd learned to put them out of her mind, never worried about them, until now. Until Fred.

'It's true I might not *mind* being married,' Eleanor admitted. 'Once upon a time. I would like a family. But never, ever with the wrong person. That would be terrible, to be trapped in that way.'

Harry nodded. She knew that all too well, after her own dismal marriage. 'What about this old friend of yours, then? Your expression just now when you mentioned him—such a soft little smile! And you'd make a wonderful countess.'

Eleanor laughed, thinking of the vast halls of Moulton

Magna, the grand gardens, the reception rooms fit to receive royalty—and how they were all starting to crumble. 'I would be a dreadful countess. I'm not nearly
grand enough.' She gave a slow, dignified wave, a distant nod, making them both giggle.

'Is this friend of yours so very *grand*, then?'

'No. Not very.' She remembered Fred chasing her
across the country meadows, his tawny hair tousled.
Carefree and simple. Not that her feelings for him had
ever been *simple*.

'Well, then…'

'It can never be, Harry, that's all.' Fred had vast responsibilities now and he needed money to fulfil them.
A lady of fortune and breeding. 'His estates are in terrible shape now. His father turned out to be a secret gambler. He needs a fortune.' A sudden, startling thought
struck her—maybe that was why he was in Bath. To
find an heiress.

'Oh, well,' Harry said. 'He is not the only fish in
Bath, Eleanor dear.'

But he was the only *fish* she might have wanted and
he was beyond her. Like the moon and stars. 'I am content as I am. Now, what about Mr Ashington who came
to see us last week? I have one or two ideas for him…'

There was a flurry of footsteps on the staircase, a
quick knock on the office door. Daisy peeked inside,
her eyes wide.

'I beg your pardon, Lady B, Miss St Aubin, but
there's a possible patron at the door,' she whispered.

Eleanor frowned as she reached for their appointment
book. 'I thought we were quite finished for the day.'

'She says she didn't write ahead, but she's an old friend who begs your assistance most urgently.' Her voice lowered even more, to an awed murmur. 'It's a *countess*.'

Harry sat up straight, making Miss Muffins bark. Their clients were usually well-off gentry, even knights and a baronet or two, but not often titled. 'A countess?'

'The Dowager Countess of Fleetwood.' Daisy held out an engraved card.

'Lady Fleetwood?' Eleanor gasped, remembering the old Earl's beautiful wife. Fred's *stepmother*.

'You know her?' Harry asked.

'She was married to the father of that man I told you about. The Earl.'

Harry's brow arched. 'Indeed? Well, Daisy, do show her in at once. And fetch some tea and some of those nice lemon cakes.'

Eleanor quickly smoothed her hair, hoping the curls weren't escaping their tight pins again, and smoothed her dark green skirt. Her heart was pounding as if she'd run a mile, to find her old life suddenly dropping into the new one.

Penelope, Lady Fleetwood, came into the room and Eleanor felt herself grow calmer. She'd only met the new Lady Fleetwood a few times before they left the vicarage but she had always been a kind, warm and welcoming presence. Even a bit shy despite her beauty and high position. Eleanor feared her years as Countess might have changed her, yet it seemed not. She was still very lovely, tall and willow-slim with shining, almost black hair just touched at the temples with a hint of silver. Her wide eyes almost matched the violet-blue of her pelisse and bonnet as she gazed around in obvious curiosity at their premises.

Eleanor remembered when Miss Penelope Preston, the widowed Mrs Elton, married the Earl. The whole neighbourhood was agog with the gossip of it. A man of his age with grown sons! And she so young, with such a small fortune. Yet the new Countess soon showed herself to be a treasure to the neighbourhood. Refurbishing the fusty old house and opening the gardens for teas and fetes. She was charitable, kind and always ready with a quick smile and polite word or act of assistance. The gossip soon became how did such a grumpy old man find such a fine wife?

After Eleanor and Mary moved away and the Earl died, everyone was shocked that he had left such vast debts and worried what might become of the dear Countess, still so young with no children of her own. She vanished from Moulton Magna, and Eleanor had heard she might be in Bath, seeking the waters, but she hadn't seen Penelope until now. Here, at their very own agency!

What could she be doing there? Perhaps she sought a wife for Fred? The thought made Eleanor long to sink through the floor and vanish.

But she couldn't. She had a business to run. She stood up with a smile and an outstretched hand. 'Lady Fleetwood. How very good to see you again.'

Penelope's smile widened with unfeigned happiness and she squeezed Eleanor's hand. 'And I am quite overjoyed to see *you*, Miss St Aubin. The church at

All Saints was never the same after your family left! I'm happy you're looking so well and what a charming premises for your work. You must be terribly busy.'

'We are indeed, yes.'

'So many people are in need of a little romance in their lives. I am glad you're here to help them.'

'We try our best.' Eleanor gestured to Harry, who watched them with curiosity. 'And this is my friend, Lady Briggs. I'm afraid Mary is out on an errand. She'll be sorry to have missed you.'

'So pleased to meet you, Lady Briggs. I hear such glorious word of your fashion. You must give me the name of your modiste now that I'm done with odious mourning. And I'm sorry to miss Mary, as well! She always livened up any gathering.'

Eleanor had to laugh. It was true that a large part of their success was due to Mary. Eleanor's sister was a born matchmaker and people person. She'd been engaged to two boys at once at the age of ten. She'd never lost the allure of her golden curls and wide, caramel-brown eyes, her ready laugh and the way she paid such close attention to anyone she spoke to, as if they were the only person in all the world. She was excellent at finding just the right people for each other, no matter how eccentric, slotting them together like perfect puzzle pieces. Eleanor had started out as more shy, more uncertain, not as instinctive. But marriage needed a pragmatic touch as well and she could do that.

Harry was a great businesswoman, organised, efficient, brisk. Adept at moving through society. Eleanor could see that shrewd speculation in Harry's eyes now as she studied Lady Fleetwood.

'Do sit down, Lady Fleetwood,' Harry said, gesturing to the cosy gathering of velvet-cushioned armchairs near the window, reserved for favourite clients. Daisy brought in the best tea set, arranging the plates and cups on a low, marble-topped table. 'Will you take tea?'

'Oh, you are kind! I don't want to take up too much of your time, if you are expecting callers,' Lady Fleetwood said. 'It was quite rude of me not to write ahead.'

'Not at all. Our books are open for the rest of the afternoon,' Eleanor said. 'I should so much enjoy hearing more of how you have been faring, Lady Fleetwood.'

'Do call me Penelope, I beg you! We're old friends and I do need as many friends as I can find right now.' She arranged the folds of her dark blue satin pelisse and smiled as Harry offered a cake. She glanced out at the cathedral, glowing mellow gold in the afternoon light. 'What a splendid view you have. One does hear such good reports of Kingston Buildings. So comfortable and so conveniently located. Do you live here as well as have your offices?'

'Mary and I have rooms upstairs and yes, it is a very comfortable situation,' Eleanor said, pouring out the tea. 'Lady Briggs lives on the Royal Crescent itself.'

'How glorious!' Penelope sighed and her gaze turned wistful as she studied the people strolling down below. 'I do wish I could join you somewhere like this. Where there must always be so much to command your attention. I am at Sunderland Street. It's not bad at all, but so short and quiet.'

Eleanor and Harry exchanged a quick glance, remembering how the houses there, though built to impress, were rumoured to be damp. The Earl's lost fortune again.

'How can we be of assistance?' Harry asked gently and passed the plate of lemon cakes from Molland's.

Penelope smiled. 'Oh, now I am afraid you will think me a horribly interfering old mama! But I hope we *are* old enough friends that I can speak with you most freely.'

'You may certainly be assured of every discretion,' Eleanor said.

'Well, you see, I am here on behalf of Frederick. The new Lord Fleetwood, my stepson.'

It was just as Eleanor had feared. Fred was looking for a wife. And she would have to find a way to watch him marry. To pretend that she did not care. That she was happy for him. How could she do that? She took a deep breath and tried to maintain an even, serene expression. 'Did Fr—? That is, did Lord Fleetwood send you here?'

Penelope looked horrified. 'No, indeed! He would not like that at all. He insists he has no need to marry. But I know—and you know, too, I am sure—that he must. I worry about him so much since he returned from Waterloo. Physically he has healed, but in his mind…' She shook her head. 'He has always been so kind to me. So welcoming when I married his father and came to Moulton Magna as scared as a goose. He often wrote to me when he was away with the Army and we became as close as a—well, perhaps not a true mother and son, but definitely as a favourite auntie of sorts. He's such a kind man. So aware of his duty now, despite how it might all appear. Despite any old gossip.'

Eleanor knew Penelope was right. *That* was not really Fred, the drinking and carousing rumours. Not *her* Fred. Her Fred was laughing and fun and kind. Now he was scarred, seemingly both inside and out, hardened. But surely her old Fred was still hidden in their somewhere.

Penelope leaned forward. 'He needs someone to help him in his new life. A wife.'

Eleanor and Harry glanced at each other again. Eleanor could see in Harry's face they would have to take this case on. Even if it broke Eleanor's heart.

'I'm sure, Lady Fleetwood,' Harry said, 'that a man such as your stepson, titled, a military hero, with a fine estate…'

Penelope gently shook her head. 'Moulton Magna is, I'm afraid, quite in dire straits. My late husband, for all his fine points, was no manager of money and the estate is in trouble. It will take much assistance to bring it to its former glory. To be honest, my dears—it will need a wife of good fortune, as well as the upbringing and spirit to oversee it all. And to put up with Fred, as he is now. Rather like a bear with a hurt paw, he does like to growl so.'

'His scars, they pain him?' Eleanor choked out.

'Not pain any more, no. But in his mind—oh, my dear Eleanor. He seems so different inside now, as well, so angry and quiet and solitary.'

Eleanor pressed her hand to her lips, trying to hold

back the tears at the idea of Fred being so unhappy, so lost.

'Is he ever—violent, Lady Fleetwood?' Harry asked carefully.

'No!' Penelope and Eleanor both protested.

'No,' Penelope went on. 'Never—except that one time he found a shepherd beating his dog and intervened most—strenuously.' Miss Muffins whined. 'I am not sure what he really saw in the war. He refuses to speak of it. He just keeps it all pressed down deep inside and I'm sure that cannot be good for him. How can he ever move forward? Find the beauty in life again?' She gazed down at the gloves in her lap, her eyes shining as if she, too, wanted to cry for him.

Eleanor's heart ached so much at the thought of Fred caught in such misery. Not her laughing, light-hearted friend. 'And you think he needs a wife?'

'Of course he does. One with a fortune, of course. Such an ancient estate, with so many people relying on it. It cannot be allowed to fall into ruin,' Penelope said firmly. 'But it's not just a wife for the estate dear Fred needs. He needs a friend, too. He would be furious to hear me say it, but he needs someone to care for him. Be kind with him. Patient. Loving and fun. As well as rich!' She laughed wryly. 'I don't ask for much, do I? It seems impossible.'

Eleanor and Harry laughed with her. They heard such lists regularly. Ones even longer and more specific and outlandish—hair colour, eye colour, the way someone pronounced 'supposedly'. Yet few from such a point of sweet, hopeful caring.

'We only take on clients of the best character here at the agency, Penelope, I promise you,' Eleanor said, 'while also keeping in mind the practicalities needed in marriage. I agree, Fred has endured so much and has a great task ahead of him still. He deserves the finest of partners. The—the best wife.' Her voice grew hoarse on that last word and she bit her lip again to hold back any ridiculous jealousy or longing.

Penelope relaxed back in her chair, the worried line between her eyes softening. 'Then you have a lady in mind?'

Harry hurried across the room to sort through one of the file drawers. She glanced at one, shook her head, moved on. Pulled a face at the next one. But soon she'd made a short, *very* short, stack of possibilities.

'Our methods are most careful,' Eleanor told Penelope. 'We almost never have a match in mind immediately. We look at the personalities and life situations of each person who comes to us very closely. What they say they desire…'

'And what they really need,' Harry said. 'Mary is especially good at winkling out that magical *something* that makes all the difference. We don't want to see our patrons merely wed, but very happy.'

Penelope clapped her hands. 'Oh, yes! I do want that so much for dear Fred. And he…' She hesitated. 'He need not know yet, if I engage your services?'

Quite against her will, Eleanor felt a tiny touch of hope deep in her heart. Fred didn't really want a wife yet? Maybe there could be some other solution to all their troubles? Yet she feared she was just being silly. Just letting hope creep in where there was none.

'I'm afraid that would be quite impossible, Penelope,' Harry said firmly. 'We have extensive interviews with every possible match, otherwise it is all too difficult. But you can definitely be with him, help him, when he speaks to us. And Eleanor and Mary already know him! It should be simple enough.'

Penelope still looked unsure and Eleanor couldn't blame her. Nothing about Fred seemed *simple*. 'I will talk to him, then. If you could have a few possible ladies to mention when we next call? If we can make him move quickly, so much the better.'

'Assuredly, yes.' Harry came back to the table to pass the cakes again. 'And what of yourself, Lady Fleetwood? Penelope.'

Penelope's hand froze reaching for a cake. 'Me, Lady Briggs?'

'Call me Harriet! Or Harry. I know we shall be great friends. Anyone Eleanor likes I definitely like and I can see you are a very good-hearted, caring person. Could you not also use the agency's services? We do have several fine gentlemen...'

'Oh, no!' Penelope cried. 'I have no thoughts of ever marrying again.'

Eleanor gave her a gentle smile. 'Are you quite sure? Any man would be so fortunate...'

Penelope laughed again. 'Oh, my dears. I am only thirty-one, but have been married twice. The first was an arrangement with the son of my father's friend—a man much given to the bottle. Fortunately, it did not last long, as he was killed racing his curricle on a bet. When my father died not long after that, there was little money and I was quite on my own until I met Fleetwood.'

Eleanor remembered the old Earl, red-faced, always irritable and another gambler to boot. He didn't sound like much of a fairy-tale rescue. 'He was also much older, I should think?'

'Yes, but he was rather settled in his ways by then. Tempted by nothing but the card tables. Too tired for other women. It was a quiet enough life, not a truly bad one and I had a home and position. Moulton Magna is a fine estate with much history and I loved being of help to the neighbourhood. And if I sometimes dreamed of something, well, more…'

Her words drifted off on a wistful smile.

'Dreamed of what, Penelope?' Eleanor urged.

Penelope gave a little wave, as if to brush away the thoughts. 'Oh, when I was young, I was very silly and romantic! I dreamed of a prince to sweep me off my feet, as young girls always do.'

'And you don't think of such things now? Maybe a younger husband?' Harry said.

'I am too old for such fancies now, I fear. I worry about Fred, that's all. Do you really think you can help him?'

'We can certainly try, Penelope,' Eleanor said, trying not to think of Fred marching down a flower-lined aisle to his beautiful, kind, rich wife. He did need a wife and it couldn't be her.

Penelope gave a relieved sigh. 'Thank you so much! I was certain I could rely on you.'

'Have Lord Fleetwood meet us at the Pump Room tomorrow morning,' Harry said. 'Just an informal greeting between old friends. We can look about and see what we all think.'

Penelope was all smiles when she took her leave and so was Harry. An earl as a patron of their agency! Such a grand thing. 'If we can find him just the right match, the perfect wife, our reputation shall be limitless!' she crowed as she danced about the office. 'Perhaps we shall have a duke on our books next.'

'Dukes would never need anyone's help to find a wife,' Eleanor argued. But even she had to smile to see her friend's joy. Harry had too little of that in the past and deserved every second. If only she could feel so excited about finding a wife for Fred. Of all people… She had to pretend to be calm, to smile, to not let anyone see the turmoil of her feelings. She was the quiet one, the reliable one. She could not let storms of emotion overcome her. Couldn't let her own feelings show.

And Harry was quite right. Matching an earl could do their business no harm at all. They were prosperous enough, it was true, but their books were mostly filled with people solidly respectable—lawyers, physicians, shopkeepers, mill owners. A few baronets who had some difficulties with shyness or eccentricity or whatever. Widows, young ladies who had passed several Seasons with no luck. Governesses and companions. There had been a milliner, who matched with the owner of a patisserie and they now created astonishingly beautiful cakes together. They were quite the rage of the town for every party.

Yet almost no nobility yet. That could be the real making of their business. If only it wasn't Fred.

'What about Miss Weston?' Harry mused, as she danced towards the files and sifted through them. 'She is so pretty and seems level-headed for one so young. Or Miss Evans from this morning? Such a fortune!'

'Miss Weston has a very small dowry,' Eleanor pointed out.

Harry frowned in thought. 'Yes, and Lady Fleetwood did say their home desperately needs a new roof. What of Mrs Gilbert? She has pots of money left from her late husband and surely Moulton Magna would have room for all her cats. How many does she have now?'

'Nearly thirty, I believe,' Eleanor sighed, picturing an army of felines traipsing up the marble staircase of Moulton Magna and scratching the parquet floors of the Long Gallery. But it was true Mrs Gilbert was wealthy and pretty. 'Is she quite young enough for children, do you think?'

'Oh, yes, the all-important heir business.' A cloud of sadness passed over Harry's lovely face for an instant. There had been no children in her own marriage. She smiled again, determined and tossed the files aside. 'We shall keep looking. We must go to the next assembly and see who has newly arrived. The Master of Ceremonies is sure to know all the freshest news.'

Harry tapped her fingertip on the ledger and went on. 'But what of Lady Fleetwood herself? She seems like prime matchmaking material. So beautiful. Such a fine dresser! And obviously caring. Look how she is concerned about her stepson.'

And Penelope seemed so sad.

Eleanor nodded. She understood why Penelope could be melancholy—two such dutiful marriages, no romance, no fun. 'Yet she says she doesn't want to marry again.'

Harry shuddered in sympathy. 'And who can blame her? The first two husbands sound dreadful! But not every match is like that at all. We should find her someone young. Someone handsome and merry…'

Daisy knocked at the door again. 'A caller for you, Lady Briggs, Miss St Aubin.'

'Ah,' Harry said, with a cat-with-the-cream kind of smile. 'Perhaps this is Lady Fleetwood's Adonis at last, heard us calling for him!'

It was not. It was Mr Parker. Eleanor sank down in her chair, barely resisting the urge to slide beneath the desk and be silent until he left.

Poor Mr Parker was one of their clients longest on the books. There was nothing really, truly objectionable about him. He was youngish, presentable if a bit on the short and balding side, possessed a prosperous estate as well as a Bath townhouse and was a good enough dancer and rider. Yet none of the ladies they'd found for him ever suited. Each meeting was an exercise in futility, as he found each lady too blonde, or too dark, too tall or too short, too talkative or too silent. If he did not pay them a very generous retention fee, Harry would surely have seen him off long ago. Eleanor wasn't entirely sure the fee was ever worth it.

At the end of every meeting, when a few new ladies' files were presented, he would sigh deeply and give Eleanor a long, sad, wounded fawn stare from his brown eyes made inhumanly large by his spectacles.

'Oh, Miss St Aubin, I do so fear *none* of them could properly suit, amiable as they all are,' he would say mournfully. 'I am expecting a lady exactly like *yourself*.'

Once in a while, patrons did come to imagine they might prefer one of the matchmakers to the matches. It was usually golden, laughing Mary or willowy, sophisticated Harry, but sometimes they glimpsed something in Eleanor they strangely preferred. Most were very easily moved along with an introduction to a lady from the files, leaving only gratitude behind. But Mr Parker was a tougher example.

He strode into the office behind Daisy and bowed low over Eleanor's reluctantly offered hand. Harry just raised her brow at them, no help at all. 'My dear, *dear* Miss St Aubin! And Lady Briggs. I do look forward to this moment every week, it is quite the brightest in my dull, sad existence.'

'Then we must draw you up out of your loneliness at last, dear Mr Parker!' Harry said with determined cheerfulness. She opened one of the files on the desk with a crisp snap. 'We have a lovely new lady. A Miss Evans…'

Mr Parker didn't take his moon-eyed gaze off Eleanor. 'Oh, no, I could not bear such a name as *Evans*.'

When he finally left, after discussing a few more possibilities, Harry tossed the files back into their drawers with a huff and some of them scattered on the floor. Miss Muffins barked in wild excitement at the unaccustomed chaos and sank her teeth into the corner of a paper.

'Impossible!' Harry cried. 'Sometimes I think you should just agree to marry the silly man yourself and get him off our books.'

Eleanor shot Harry a horrified glare that made Harry's frown turn into laughter. 'Not really, my dear, of course! How could Mary and I stand him as part of our little family? All his delicate little niceties to you, ugh. If only we could find him someone else!'

'We've tried everyone, really. And poor Miss Evans doesn't deserve that after living with her mother all her life.'

'True, true. Well, once we find a wife for the Earl, our coffers will overflow and we won't need Mr Parker's retainer. Now, let's dig deep into these files and find at least a few prospects who could be a countess before we go to the Pump Room tomorrow.'

Eleanor nodded. She vowed not to be tempted by Fred again. Not by his smiles, his sadness, the way he looked at her as if he understood all she hid in her heart and soul—no, not even by that. He was a patron only now, that was all. She wouldn't think about his sky-blue eyes. The touch of his hand…

Oh, no. She had to summon up every bit of professional calm she'd learned in running the agency. She had to conceal any emotion she had for Fred. She had to do what she did best. Be a businesswoman.

She was surely doomed.

Chapter Five

'I visited Miss St Aubin yesterday,' Penelope announced ever so casually over the breakfast table. She reached for the toast rack and a jar of marmalade and pushed them towards Fred. 'You should eat more, Fred dearest! The doctors say you must build up your strength.'

'I'm going with you to the Pump Room to drink those waters of hellfire, isn't that enough?' he grumbled. But really he only heard, only thought about, the first part of her statement. She had seen Eleanor.

His Eleanor. But not really *his*, never his. Only part of a dreamy, golden past. And a beautiful woman in the present.

He'd spent every moment since then trying to forget about her. About that past and all the things that could no longer be. And now here she was, in Bath, appearing like a tempting, rose-scented ghost even at his breakfast table.

'Don't tell me you went to that so-called agency of theirs,' he said.

Penelope's eyes widened in a too-innocent fashion

and she busied herself with spreading butter on her toast. 'Can I not call on old neighbours? It would be impolite not to and the St Aubin girls were always so kind.'

'So you were merely renewing an old acquaintance?' he said suspiciously.

Penelope tried to look even *more* innocent, but it didn't work so well. 'Well—we might have chatted a tiny bit about their work. So fascinating! Ladies making their own way in this harsh world. And such a helpful service they render.'

He tossed down his fork in exasperation. Everything in the world seemed determined to conspire to throw him in the path of Eleanor, when the pain of seeing her, longing to touch her, kiss her, absorb all her gentleness and warmth into his cold heart, was overwhelming. 'Pen! If I was going to seek out a wife, which I am not at present, I would do so myself. No need to involve the St Aubins.'

Penelope gave him a beseeching smile. 'But you refuse to seek out any ladies at all! You lurk about the house. Won't meet with anyone. Won't go to plays or assemblies. There is a masked fete at Sydney Gardens in a few weeks that would be perfect and you won't attend with me! You stomp in and out of the Pump Room quite like an old bear, sweeping out without conversing with anyone. This is no way to meet nice young ladies.'

'What nice young lady would want to talk to me at all?' He gestured towards his scarred cheek, his burned hand. 'I am hardly a picture of beauty. No lady wants this. Even I do not like looking in the mirror.'

Penelope's smile turned sympathetic. 'Many more ladies than you would think. Your scars have greatly faded under the doctors' treatment and you know your title and estate are a fine offering. You used to be so— so...' She broke off with a sigh.

'I used to be?' he said quietly.

'Such good fun. Always laughing. Always understanding and comforting. Always ready to be a friend. Of course, we all get older and more sedate...'

'So I am sedate now?' he said teasingly. She wasn't entirely wrong. He well remembered those days of exploring the woods with Eleanor, chasing through the fields, reading poetry, coming up with dreams and jokes. But even Eleanor seemed quiet now, her burdens bearing down on her as his did on him. He felt such a cold wave of sadness at losing that joy. At the way life had damaged him. 'Where is my stick? My bath chair? I require a nurse, not a wife!'

Penelope laughed. 'Not *quite* in your extreme dotage, maybe. But you must be careful. The years slip by before you know it, and your dreams have fled entirely.' She looked down at the damask tablecloth, her eyes shadowed as if she was lost in her own memories. Fred couldn't help but wonder if she could use the agency herself. She deserved love and happiness.

'You were such a merry lad when I first wed your father,' she continued, 'you brightened the gloomy halls of Moulton Magna to no end. I know that man is still in there, demanding to be free again.'

'I think I left him at Waterloo,' he said. That was a moment in his life he'd long wanted to forget. A moment that haunted his nightmares. But now, with her, he was surprised to discover the memories had begun to fade. He'd suspected Eleanor, the Eleanor he'd once known, could bring him out again, that joyful man. But there was not a chance of that now.

'You should not underestimate yourself, Fred,' she said. 'Just talk to Eleanor St Aubin! Their agency seems terribly well-organised, so efficient and they care so much about helping people find happiness. They could save you a great deal of trouble. Find a few suitable ladies for you to at least meet.'

Against his will, Fred felt a frisson of intrigue at her words. 'You had a peek at their files, then?'

Penelope shook her head regretfully. 'I should have so enjoyed that! Like a novel come to life. But they are quite locked up tight. Their rates are very reasonable. A small retainer, then the remainder on marriage. Everything always most proper and chaperoned. They could save us much time.'

'Time before the roof caves in on us?'

'Perhaps. Yes, to be brutally honest.' She reached across the table and gently squeezed his hand. 'Just have a chat with Eleanor. You and she were once good friends, I think. She can surely help us.'

He sighed. He knew Penelope, kind as she was, would not let go of a thought to help someone once it was in her head. And Moulton Magna did need a mistress. 'I only said we would call on them.'

'Excellent! Because I believe they may be at the Pump Room this morning. Now, eat up your marmalade. It's your favourite, sent from Molland's.'

Fred took a bite of his toast and had to admit it *was* excellent marmalade. Perhaps he was starting to enjoy a bit of the world after all, even against his will. Maybe the old Fred was still in there, just as Pen suggested. Just as Eleanor had once brought out in him.

'Such a lovely day! Not a drop of rain in the sky,' Mary said in delight as they made their way towards the Pump Room. They journeyed there nearly every morning, to peruse the book of arrivals for possible new patrons, study the crowds and check on the progress on some of their matched couples.

It didn't quite feel like an ordinary day, though. No days were ordinary since Eleanor had seen Fred again.

'No rain,' she murmured. 'Most unusual for Bath.'

'And smell that breeze! Bath buns baking, flowers on the stalls again, sunshine and light.' Mary took Eleanor's arm and drew in a deep breath, the pink feathers on her chop straw bonnet fluttering. Several young men turned to stare at her, but she ignored them. 'It's warm and bright now, perfect for romance. And you also look so pretty today, Ella.'

Eleanor self-consciously tugged at the scalloped hem of her new pale blue taffeta pelisse. She *had* dressed rather carefully that morning, in a white gown sprigged with blue flowers and blue moire ribbons fluttering from her bonnet, a colour she hoped suited her dark curls and pale skin. She always dressed neatly and stylishly for their work, of course. But she usually didn't think of fashion beyond that, as Mary and Harry did. She couldn't compete with Harry's elegance or Mary's porcelain shepherdess prettiness. Today, though, she'd been at the dressing table longer than usual.

She didn't want to admit the real reason was the possibility of seeing Fred again.

'Ah, Miss St Aubin! Miss Mary!' a voice called as they turned towards the portico of the Pump Room. 'So pleased to see you this morning.'

Eleanor plastered her most pleasant, professional smile on her lips and turned to greet Lady Hastings and her daughter. The Hastings were a new addition to the agency's books—a baronet's widow and her daughter. Miss Hastings had been through two London Seasons, was pretty and quite spry, unlike quiet Miss Evans, but her father had been a fisherman's son of all things and so many high sticklers turned up their nose at her. Yet her mama, much like Mrs Evans, wanted *only* high sticklers for her only daughter. A viscount at best and she guarded stringently against title-less fortune-hunters. As did the agency, of course. Their network of discreet investigators looked closely at any and all possible scoundrels.

Yet Miss Hastings seemed to find the careful process rather vexing and Eleanor worried about her impetuous ways. She remembered too well how romantic poetry gave a young lady dreamy ideas, especially since Fred came back into her life. Yes, it was best to find Miss Hastings a match as soon as possible.

She was all smiles today, though, pert and pretty under her pink, ruffled bonnet.

Mary took Eleanor's arm as they waved greetings to the Hastings ladies and continued into the Pump Room.

'Perhaps Miss Hastings might do for Fred!' Mary whispered eagerly.

Eleanor tried not to show her shock, her sudden pang at those words. 'For Fred?'

'Indeed. She has a fine fortune. Her mother wants a title for her. She is young and lively and does not seem to have a particular romantic attachment as yet. Perhaps she could help brighten up Moulton Magna for him!'

Eleanor started to protest, but she had to admit Mary did have a point. Miss Hastings was young, pretty and rich. It didn't matter how much the thought of Fred marching up the aisle with Miss Hastings pained her. It could not matter.

'We must persuade him to officially sign as a patron of the agency first, which I think might be no easy task,' Eleanor said.

'I am quite sure Lady Fleetwood can persuade him.' Mary glanced back thoughtfully at Miss Hastings. 'Harry says Lady Fleetwood is ever so pretty and amiable! Still young, too. And married twice. So sad. Perhaps we could be of help to her, too. Two for one!'

'Penelope would certainly be an easier prospect than Fred,' Eleanor agreed. 'Yet perhaps she does now *want* to marry again, after two such trials. It can't have been easy being married to Fred's father.'

Mary shivered. She had been young when they left the vicarage, but she remembered the Earl and the way the household was back then. 'Indeed. She deserves someone handsome and romantic this time!'

They joined the line to peruse the arrivals book, nodding to friends and to old patrons who strolled past in pairs, arm in arm, examining the fashions around them as they moved through the elegant, airy pale green and cream room, with its domed ceiling and columns. The sound of harp music filled the flower-scented air.

'Oh, look, it's Mr and Mrs Shipton!' Mary whispered excitedly. 'Don't they just look radiant with happiness?'

They did indeed. The Shiptons were one of the agency's great success stories. A romance at first sight when they were introduced. They had bonded over their mutual passion for collecting antique milk pails.

'The Misses St Aubin! How grand to see you today,' Mr Simpson, the Master of Ceremonies who controlled much of bath's social life, greeted them as they stepped inside. 'So many new arrivals, as you can see, all of them vying to be entertained.'

'So I see, Mr Simpson,' Eleanor said as she scanned the lines of names in the visitors' book.

'Mr Parker was just here, enquiring about you,' Mr Simpson said softly.

Eleanor glanced back in alarm. 'I do hope you did not—that is…'

He tapped the side of his nose. 'I said I had no indication you would be visiting us this morning and I believe he ventured off to a coffee house instead.'

Eleanor sighed in relief. She wasn't sure she could quite deal with Mr Parker today. Not after a sleepless night plagued with memories of Fred.

'That was kind of you, Mr Simpson,' she said.

'But I do hope nothing will frighten you away from

our little masquerade in Sydney Gardens. It shall be quite the event,' Mr Simpson said.

'Oh, no! We wouldn't miss it for anything,' Mary cried. Mary adored any ball, especially one that involved costumes.

They bowed to Mr Simpson and made their way into the midst of the crowd. It was the way of every morning in Bath. Meet with people drinking their daily glasses of mineral water, sip tea, chat, hear the news, then perhaps go on to take the heated baths, walk and shop. Above all, they had to find possible patrons for the agency.

Near the long tables dispensing the all-essential waters, Eleanor glimpsed Fred, half hidden by a blue satin window drapery. He scowled down into his half-empty glass as if he would toss the foul stuff across the room and she could not blame him one bit. It tasted like old eggs, no one liked it, of course. But he also looked as if he longed to make a joke of it all, as the old Fred would have and she couldn't help but laugh.

She pressed her gloved fingertips to her lips to hold back a snort of laughter, but he heard her anyway. He glanced up and actually gave her a *wink* and a white, naughty, wide, flashing smile. A conspiracy just between the two of them in the middle of the crowd. That smile that was always able to fell a lady at fifty paces. To make her long to dash across a ballroom and throw himself at her feet, begging her to be his.

Eleanor hadn't seen that smile in so long and never directed right at her. She had been young when they were friends and he had no rakish reputation then. For an instant, she was frozen, couldn't breathe at all. It had been so very long since she saw that old, wonderful Fred. He hadn't changed so very much, maybe. A fantasy come to life, brave and funny and with those gorgeous lapis eyes. Tall, self-possessed, making a lady long to just stand and stare and dream.

He poured away the last of the water into a potted palm and held his finger to his lips to beg her silence. A little secret between them. Eleanor made a zipping motion.

Someone bumped into Fred and said a few words to him, making him turn away. When he glanced at Eleanor again, her light-hearted Fred was gone once more, and the wounded bear warrior was there. She turned away, flustered. How wonderful it had been to see him again, to know he was really there. And then just to lose him again! She blinked hard against the prickle of tears, praying no one noticed.

'Oh, look, Eleanor, there is Lord Fleetwood himself! We should say hello,' Mary said and forged ahead as she always did. There was never stopping her.

Eleanor followed more slowly, trying to keep smiling, keep serene, nodding to acquaintances. Trying to pretend today was the same as any other day at the Pump Room. As if her world, the world she'd so carefully built around her, hadn't cracked and collapsed with Fred's return.

Luckily, by the time they reached Fred's side, Penelope had joined him and Eleanor didn't have to face him quite alone.

'Well met, indeed!' Penelope declared. She set her

own nearly full glass on a footman's tray and smiled at them brightly. 'Fred, dearest, you do recall the Misses St Aubin, I'm sure. It's been so delightful to find you will be our neighbours again. I declare I have been quite lonely since coming to Bath.'

'Indeed. Delightful. A surprise,' Fred said wryly. Eleanor noticed he kept his damaged hand close to his side, half hidden by his sleeve and her heart ached to see it.

'Miss Mary, I do adore your hat,' Penelope said brightly, distracting Eleanor from Fred. 'You must tell me where you found it. I must replenish my wardrobe after all this dull mourning. Do walk with me and let us chat?' She gave Fred a long glance. 'Fred, darling, do take the waters as the doctors said. A pint a day, remember?'

Penelope and Mary strolled off arm in arm, chatting merrily about hats and pelisses, leaving Eleanor to stand alone with Fred. 'You must take a *pint*?' she said, appalled.

Fred grimaced. 'Indeed. Pen has dragged me to several physicians and apothecaries and their advice does not seem to vary. Sadly.'

'I am quite convinced the doctors are in the pay of this very Pump Room itself and someone down in the cellars must add something to the water to make people feel *worse*. Then everyone must put their coin into longer and longer stays here.'

'Your theory has merit, Ella.'

Ella again. His special name for her. 'I know where

we can procure some cups of perfectly decent tea, if you like? What Penelope doesn't know and all that…'

Fred gave a blissful sigh and that wonderful old smile again. 'You are an angel, Ella. Do lead on.'

He offered her his good arm and she slowly slid her fingers over his sleeve, hardly believing they were there together once more. His arm felt solid, strong and hard under her touch. They made their way around the edge of the room towards the tea tables, silent together. She reminded herself sternly that she still had to find him a wife. That this could not last. But, at least, there was this moment. This comfort and ease.

'Are you—that is, do you have to see so many doctors, then?' she asked carefully, trying to not show her worry.

He shrugged, his muscles rippling under her hand. 'There is not so much they can do for me. I am as I shall be and I do not feel so terrible. Just a twinge of soreness now and then. Not a thing to worry about.' He flashed that smile down at her, making her feel warm and glowing all over again even as she feared he might just be putting on a brave face for her. 'And there is my wounded vanity, of course.'

Eleanor laughed. 'You always did have a surfeit of that.'

'Oh, you *do* wound me! How insufferable I must have been when I was young.'

'Indeed you were. Yet I did miss you when you were gone,' she admitted. 'The neighbourhood became terribly dull.'

'And I missed you,' he said quietly, making her cheeks feel warm. He had thought of her!

'I'm surprised you tolerate the Bath doctors, then,' Eleanor said.

'It gives Penelope a certain pleasure to fuss and I want to make sure she's happily settled here before I return to Moulton Magna,' he answered. 'She worries.'

Eleanor did not blame her. It was easy to worry about Fred, who'd always hidden any pain. 'She seems like a very kind lady.'

'Too good a lady for my father,' he answered. 'I have to say, Ella, I know she has visited you in your—professional capacity recently.' He gave a little cough, sounding almost embarrassed to mention the agency.

Eleanor swallowed hard. Did he think less of her for her work? 'I am sure she only wants to be of assistance.'

He smiled, that old, quirked, smile of his once more and Eleanor's heart dangerously stuttered. 'I am quite sure of that.'

'I'd like to be of assistance, too. To help you be—be happy,' Eleanor said softly, with such a pang that some other lady would make him happy in that way. She almost reached out to touch his hand, but curled her fingers tightly to hold herself back. Helping him in his matrimonial quest was never going to be an easy thing, she knew that, but it was proving more difficult than she'd imagined. Harder to keep her feelings for him hidden. 'If not through the agency, then as an old friend. With advice and such. If I can.'

He glanced away out of the window and was silent for a long moment. She longed to know what he was thinking. What he truly wanted. 'I know I must wed. My father left things rather in a muddle and it's my duty now. But to use an agency...' he shook his head. 'Forgive me if I have my doubts.'

'You could call it a muddle, yes,' Eleanor said with a sympathetic grimace. She thought of the shocked letters they had received from old friends, once the Earl died and the extent of his debts was revealed. Moulton Magna had always seemed the centre of their neighbourhood, their anchor. 'I assure you, though, our agency is completely above board and most professional.'

'Yet who would have me as I am now?' he said. He sounded matter-of-fact, even half joking, with not a speck of self-pity but just a certain reality.

'You are more handsome than you ever knew, Fred,' she blurted.

He glanced down at her quizzically. 'And you are a good friend, Ella. Better than I ever deserved. I wasted any attractions I might once have had in being a ridiculous wastrel. I wasted anything that might have been worthy of your friendship. And now...'

Now he had to marry a fortune. 'You must do your duty, which is something I understand very well.' For hadn't she, too, done her duty? Left school, taken care of her father, their home, her sister, their patrons at the agency. Forgotten about those days running free with Fred. Surely she should be able to keep those parts of herself separate in her heart. If he could do that, so she could she.

She made herself look away from him to glance

around the room at all the ladies gathered there. There were so many countess candidates in Bath. Young ladies of fine dowries, pretty faces, even kind hearts. Yet who was right for Fred? Who could be worthy of him?

'You have a professional look in your eye right now, Ella,' he teased. 'Have you a candidate in mind right now?'

'Ah, well, you must pay the agency's fee if you want to know,' she answered, trying to be light-hearted, to hide all her old feelings for him, her memories and silly half-hopes. All her thoughts about him now, in this moment.

He laughed, suddenly looking so much younger, lighter. As if being with her made the years vanish for him as they did for her. 'Quite right. Well, then, shall we take a turn about the room and look for Pen and your sister? You can tell me all I must know about how to make my way properly around Bath. I fear I have quite turned feral of late. Too quiet. Too much inside myself.'

Yet Eleanor had heard once that that was not true. That he'd gone rather wild with ladies and gambling, maybe after all the horrors he'd seen in war. Then the quiet feral ways, as he called it, were a way to dull the pain, too. How she wished she could bring him into the sunshine once again! That they could be free together once more.

He offered her his arm and she hesitated a moment before she slid her hand over his sleeve, fearing she might never want to let him go. When she did, she found he felt just like the old Fred—and like something new, something enticing and strong and, yes, hard to let go. 'Stay with me then, Fred, and you shan't lose your way in Bath.' Though she very well might.

Chapter Six

Ella often liked to venture out early on a fine morning, before Mary and Harry had even left their dressing tables. She loved the cool, calm silence before the rest of the town came to life. She and Miss Muffins would buy a tea and a Bath bun and stroll by the river to watch the water meander and twist along on its voyage. She sometimes wondered where it went, after it left Bath. What it saw. A few fishermen were there, catching their day's wares, and some housemaids were collecting the day's provisions. Otherwise, Ella was alone for a short, precious time.

She nibbled her Bath bun as she studied the pale morning sunlight, the small crafts that slipped past in the water, and let the blessed silence surround her. No one demanded she find them their 'One True Love For Ever' right now, no account books awaited. She could just breathe, take in the bridge and the water and the lights. And think.

Think about this new Fred. Ella sighed to consider it. Once, long ago, she'd thought she knew him well. But now—now she was sure she didn't know him at all. This Fred was harder, sharper-edged, more cynical than the young man she'd once known. He did not laugh as he once did. Did not enjoy the parties. Worry had carved new lines in his face, even beyond the scars.

Could she come to incorporate this new Fred into her old memories, her friend? She ached for what he'd suffered. Longed to help him even as he seemed to hold her apart. What could she do? She so longed for her friend again. The distance he put between them made her want to cry, to wail, to let out all the emotion she kept so carefully hidden. She wanted to wrap her arms around him and never let him go. To be with him always.

Miss Muffins seemed to whine in agreement.

They were suddenly interrupted by Ella's sister calling her name. 'Ella! There you are at last. You quite vanished.'

Mary glanced over her shoulder to smile at her sister, who hurried along the pier in the shade of her lacy parasol. 'Such a splendid day, Eleanor, don't you agree?' Mary declared, as they stepped from their door into the sunny morning. She popped open her lacy parasol, shielding them from the unaccustomed glare after so many grey afternoons. 'How I wish we could be out in nature somewhere, instead of going to the shops. Do you remember the woods at Moulton Magna, when we were children? How gloriously free it all was.'

'Indeed I do,' Eleanor said with a secret little smile, as she remembered running with Fred through those light-dappled woods. 'Living here in Bath has so many fine things—concerts and theatres, bookshops and milliners—but I do sometimes miss the quiet of the woods and paths, as well.'

They linked arms and turned towards York Street. They peeked into shop windows at ribbons and slippers, leather-bound books and lengths of fabric, greeted friends and chatted about new patrons.

'My dear Eleanor! Mary!' they heard a lady call as they headed towards the Gardens. Eleanor glanced back to see an open landau rolling to a halt near them, Lady Fleetwood and Fred seated inside. She had not seen him since the Pump Room and encountering him again so unexpectedly made her feel all warm and confused. So ridiculously young, as only Fred could do.

'How lovely to see you again,' Penelope said. 'And on such a fine day! Fred has taken the waters this morning…'

Eleanor gave Fred a sympathetic grimace, remembering how much of the sulphurous waters he was meant to consume, which made him laugh.

'So we hired this carriage for the day,' Penelope went on, pretending not to see his chuckles. 'The doctor says fresh air and exercise can be of great benefit, so we're off to Beechen Cliff for a picnic. There are great views to be had, I'm sure. They say there are ruins there! Maybe even a castle. I love a fine view of a ruin, don't you, Fred dear?'

'Oh, assuredly,' he said quickly and shot a glance at Eleanor, his brow quirked. It was her turn to laugh aloud, quickly smothered by her gloved hand.

'It sounds like a place in a poem,' Mary said wistfully. 'We haven't been able to venture out to the hills beyond town much of late.'

'Then you must come with us!' Penelope declared. 'I'm sure the doctors would tell Fred he would also benefit from time with friends, going about in society. He's become such a solitary old thing.'

Eleanor peeked at Fred from under the brim of her bonnet. *Solitary old thing* would never have described the old Fred at all. That Fred was always ready for a mischief. Now she feared she could see it there, that new loneliness, in incipient lines on his face, the grimace as Pen pointed that out. Perhaps he, too, wanted to leave that loneliness behind.

She longed more than anything to make him smile again. 'I do wonder if the climb would be too much...' she ventured, thinking of the steep pathways and the old wooden stairs at Beechen Cliff.

'I am sure it would not be. Oh, Eleanor, let's go with them!' Mary cried, giving Eleanor the melting, beseeching look that always swayed her when it came to her little sister. 'It is too fine a day to stay in town.'

Eleanor glanced about uncertainly. She didn't want to make a fool of herself if she was too long in Fred's presence, as she feared she might.

Mary squeezed her arm and whispered, 'And we can find out more of what Lord Fleetwood looks for in a wife! It will help us find him a perfect match.'

'I...' Eleanor began. She did want to be with Fred. Of course she did. She had to grab any moment she could with him! But could she conceal her feelings for quite so long? Chat about possible matches for him as if she worried about nothing else?

'Please, do come with us,' Fred said with a wonderful, coaxing smile. 'If only to give Pen another focus for her infernal fussing.'

'Yes, of course,' Eleanor said. She could not refuse that smile. 'Thank you. We would enjoy that very much.'

Penelope clapped her hands. 'Wonderful! How serendipitous to see you here today.'

The footman jumped down to open the door, but Fred alighted first and held out his hand to Eleanor. 'There is a seat here, Ella,' he said, gesturing to the spot next to his own place.

'Th-thank you.' She accepted his hand and let him assist her into the carriage. He helped Mary to sit next to Penelope and he pressed close to Eleanor as the door closed and the carriage jolted back into motion. He did smell the same as the old Fred, of sunlight and warmth and all delightful things. She longed to lean against him and feel him against her. She moved closer to the door on her other side.

But she felt half silly, being so very careful around Fred. In the light of day, a grown, sensible woman with many responsibilities and Fred could be a valuable patron for her agency. She knew that very well and wanted to help him, to be a good friend to him. To see the world as it was, not as she might have once dreamed it could be and do what must be done. Yet whenever she touched his hand, whenever he was close to her, she became a dreamy, giggly girl.

She thought of the rumours that Fred had gone rather wild in London, known many women, frequented gaming halls. Eleanor knew she couldn't quite compete with women like that. She knew much about human nature, she'd based her business on it, but of the marrying sort. Fred was still very handsome and had once been gorgeous beyond belief. She suddenly wondered if he thought her silly. If he compared her with them. If he sought a woman like those he'd once known as a wife...

The carriage lurched around a corner, towards the banks of the Avon River and the road that would lead away from the town, up a steep slope and Eleanor fell against Fred's shoulder. He took her arm to hold her steady, looking down at her with a dark, inscrutable look in his eyes. She straightened her bonnet and gave him a quick, rueful smile.

'Now, do tell us about the masquerade they say will soon be held in Sydney Gardens,' Penelope said as the crowds fell away around them and they bounced over a bridge. 'It sounds quite marvellous! I haven't been to a real ball in ages.'

'Oh, yes, everyone will be there,' Mary answered with great enthusiasm. She'd been planning costumes for several weeks already. 'There will be fireworks! And music—a famous soprano.'

'Then we must obtain tickets, Fred,' Penelope said. 'A dance would do us both good. And you need a new evening suit anyway. You shall be sadly out of fashion.'

'You must resign yourself, I fear,' Eleanor told him, all mock solemnity. 'You are in Bath now, Fred. Clothes must be commissioned. Fun must be had. It's the way of the town.'

Fred grimaced and then laughed. 'So I am discovering. As long as this masquerade doesn't involve drinking yet more water…'

'I'm sure there will be champagne instead,' Mary sighed. 'And so very much dancing! Royal musicians are coming all the way from London.'

'So, along with a new suit of clothes, I must procure some dancing lessons,' Fred said.

'I remember you were a very fine dancer,' Eleanor blurted. Once they had shared a country dance at the village assembly rooms and she had dreamed of it for so long after. The touch of his hand, the way they moved together.

'You danced with Fred?' Penelope asked. 'And yet he tries to declare he has *never* danced.'

'When we were young, at a village assembly,' Eleanor said. 'He was a much sought-after partner!'

'I'm sure we can find many amiable ladies who would be delighted to have you as a partner,' Mary said. The town spread far below them, honey-gold in the sunlight, beyond the vivid green of the trees.

Staring down at the sparkle of the glorious view before her, Eleanor stumbled a bit as she descended the carriage steps. Fred caught her before she could tumble down, lifting her high for an instant as she held tight to his shoulders, staring up in wonder at his familiar, unfamiliar, beautiful face.

He slowly, ever so slowly lowered her to the ground, a gentle slide, his gaze never leaving hers. Eleanor didn't want to let him go, yet the chatter of Penelope and Mary as they made their way up the path, the chirping song of the birds, pulled her back into the real world again.

She stepped back, flustered. 'Thank you. So clumsy of me.'

'The last thing you could ever be, Ella, is clumsy,' he said hoarsely. She noticed him running his damaged arm, as if he had wrenched it and didn't want her to notice. She felt so shy and awful that he had to worry about such things now! Her strong, funny old friend.

They walked together behind Penelope and Mary and the footmen, towards a spot where they could spread out their picnic with the glorious view all around them. Eleanor lost herself in the chatter, the wine and laughter and soon felt easy again, as if she was with the old Fred and was the old Eleanor, reading poetry in the Moulton Magna summerhouse. He'd known those women in London and she'd been immured with her family. How well could they know each other now? Especially as she so feared to show him her real emotions. Her real heart.

They were not those young, innocent people still. Not really. And there was a new, taut awareness she could not deny. He was at the other end of the blanket, far from her reach, yet Eleanor was achingly aware of him at every moment. As they finished their repast and grew quiet and drowsy in the sunlight, he glanced towards her and smiled.

'Shall we walk a bit, Ella?' he asked, popping a last

strawberry into his mouth. 'I fear if I sit here any longer, I'll quite go to sleep in this delightfully warm sun.'

Eleanor hesitated. She feared what could happen, how her feelings might escape, if she was alone with him again.

'Oh, yes, do,' Penelope urged. 'Mary and I shall just chatter on here for a bit and finish this wine. You two should go look for the ruins.'

She slowly took Fred's hand as he offered to help her to her feet and blinked as the sun behind his bright hair dazzled her. They made their way away from the picnic blanket, into the shade of a narrow pathway that led between trees and flowering shrubs, smelling fresh and sweet in the warm day. They walked in silence. Comfortable, comforting and close together, until they reached a cliff that looked down on the town between a break in the greenery. It all glowed and shimmered, just like Fred. Just like that moment she had with him.

He seemed to feel it, too, studying the view with a solemn, thoughtful expression on his face. 'For whatsoever from one place doth fall, if with the tide unto another brought. For there is nothing lost, that may be found, if sought.'

'Such beautiful words of Spenser's,' she whispered.

'They always make me think of you,' he said, his gaze so very blue and intense as he studied her. 'You are like a fairy queen.'

Eleanor stared up at him, wondering if the sun had dazzled her senses, sent her flying into another realm. He thought of her as fairy queen. She knew this moment between them, very still, sparkling, a time out of time, could not last; it would vanish like all dreams. Yet his compliments, the admiration in his eyes, made her feel so warm and glowing all the way to her toes.

'Me?' she whispered. 'A fairy queen?'

'Yes. Beautiful and kind. Someone for us mere mortals to look up to in admiration. But even better. For *you*, Ella, are real. You are kind and warm.'

He suddenly took her gloved hand in his, holding it very tightly. She curved her fingers around his, holding onto him as if he was the only thing that kept her from flying away.

'See?' he said, staring down intently at their joined hands. He sounded tense, hoarse. As if he was filled with some pain, some longing, just as she was. As if he was faced with something he reverenced and feared all at once. 'Warm and real. Not an icy queen at all. You always had such a kindness about you. Like a fireside on a winter's day. A place to curl up and stay, to be safe.' He pressed her hand close against his chest and she could feel the beat of his heart through linen and wool. As if it moved through her whole self and became a part of her.

'And so are you, Fred, though I know you never give yourself such credit. You are such a wonderful friend. So…' So wonderful. She'd always thought that and now she found it had not changed.

'I can only be that way with you, Ella,' he whispered. 'Once, I…'

Eleanor stared up at him, entranced, flooded with a bittersweet longing she'd never known before. She felt so dizzy. As if the whole world shifted and changed and rocked around her. As if there was hope and fear all at once. She dared to give in to all those feelings she'd long had for Fred and leaned closer to him, resting her forehead against his shoulder. It was so warm, that heat surrounding her, blanketing her against the world. He smelled of lemon soap and clean linen, of sunshine and Fred. And, for that moment, she didn't feel alone at all.

'What could bring us back to that, Fred?' she said.

His arms came around her, close and warm and she peeked up at him to see that he stared out over the hills, as if as lost as she was amid that honey-golden glow. Lost in their own world together. 'I know I went rather wild when I first went into the Army.'

Eleanor hadn't expected such memories as that. She gave a surprised little hiccough of laughter and thought of the gossip that had once reached her ears. Tales of cards and debts, women and whisky. She had always tried to ignore it all. Discount it and hold on only to her Fred. 'I may have heard a word or two.'

'It is true, I fear. I hate to think of it now. But once the regiment left England, I became friends with another young officer. A most amiable man who hadn't been married two years yet and had a new child. He talked so often of his wife and baby in the long, lonely evenings and I—I confess I began to see another way of being through his words. A real home. A place to belong. Someone who waited for me.' He'd sounded very far away just then, sad, and Eleanor ached for him.

She squeezed his arm, pressing close to his side. She only wanted to reassure him, to rush to tell him that he could indeed have that. Could have a home, a family, anything he desired.

She could help him find that with the agency. Even if she couldn't help him in the way her heart so longed for, help him by making that home, that family together. By comforting him always.

'And your friend?' she asked. 'Did he return to his home?'

Fred shook his head, staring out over the view. 'He was killed in battle. I glimpsed him, through the haze of smoke. I tried to save him, but I was too late. I went to call on his wife as soon as I returned to England, after I had been wounded. She was going back to her parents in Jersey. She was so brave, so kind, trying to reassure *me*, when I was the one who owed her so much. Her husband should have been there, not me.' He smiled down at her, sad, wistful. She could tell he tried to hide his emotions from her, but she was too long practised in reserve herself. She could see the raw torment in his eyes. Hear the anguish of that moment. 'She rather reminded me of you, Ella.'

'Of me?' she whispered.

'Yes. So very brave, such a warm heart. I've never forgotten her and her husband. Nor can I really forget the terrors of battle, though I try to hide that from Pen. But now—now I think I begin to forget a bit.'

She studied the trees around them. The green and gold. The sky arching overhead with only birdsong to be heard. 'Is this not the most peaceful place? A place for renewal, I think.'

'Yes.' He took a deep breath and stared up at the treetops. 'Peaceful indeed.'

'If only we could live in a hut right here in the hills. All alone in the quiet, with just the sky and these trees. Like shepherds in a poem!' They were quiet together for a long moment, standing close as they took in the view below them. Only the two of them in that never-ending, too-brief moment.

'Shall we take another turn along the path before we leave?' he said at last. Eleanor nodded and silently they made their way back along the trail they'd just trod. But it was no heavy, uncomfortable silence. It was peaceful, easy, filled with birdsong and the whisper of the wind in the trees. And he held her hand close in his, helping her over slippery patches of moss and loose stones.

'What of you, Ella? What did you do when I was gone? I know setting up your agency could not have been easy,' he asked.

Eleanor laughed, thinking of those days. 'We had nothing to copy, really, no business plan before us. We just had to rely on our good sense and on Harry's fine taste. We knew we were needed. So many people come here to Bath wishing to marry!'

'Then it must be easy for them to find each other?'

'Sometimes it is, of course. With so many assemblies and tea parties! Yet there are those who seek a bit—well, more. It is easy enough to marry, but it can be so hard to find the *right* person. Especially if one is a bit…er…different.'

'I think I see. Some people are not made exactly for

this world. They need help to find someone to see them through it all. Someone to understand.'

'Yes! Their missing half. And not all our patrons are wealthy. Some save up their coin—we see merchants, governesses, milliners. We sometimes give them a bit of a bargain rate, I admit. They deserve to find someone they can care for, too.'

'Lost causes, eh?'

'No one is a lost cause. I have never believed that.'

'Not even me?' he said ruefully.

Eleanor held his hand tight and studied his face. 'Especially not you, Fred. Never you.'

'You would certainly change your mind, Ella, if you knew how I have really changed lately. You would not wish to be my friend at all.'

'That is not true!' Ella declared stoutly. She remembered what she had determined before, that time changed everyone. Especially those like Fred who were unfortunate even to see war itself. Yet knowing that only increased her understanding of him and made her feel even deeper for him. Admire his strength that much more.

'I am always here, Fred, if you need someone to talk to,' she said. 'Whether you decide to partake of our excellent services at the agency after all. I am still your friend, always.'

Fred reached for her hand and placed a warm, tingling, alluring touch to her fingers that made her shiver. 'You have no idea how very much that means to me, Ella. No idea at all.'

She smiled up at him, tremulously, and hoped that this friendship could truly be enough.

'I think I may do something shockingly naughty now,' she dared to whisper, remembering the old days with Fred, the pranks they would sometimes get up to.

He tilted his head. There was a most intrigued gleam in his eyes. 'I can't wait to hear what that might be, Ella.'

'Remember when we were young and there was that enormous ancient oak out near the summerhouse?'

He nodded, looking doubtful but also interested, maybe even a bit excited.

'That tree over there looks very similar,' she said. 'I think I shall climb it, like I used to.'

His expression slid into doubt and that only made her feel more determined. 'Ella. I'm not sure that's a good idea.'

'You think I don't have it in me any longer?' she teased. If they were to be friends, she wanted it to be just as it was. Free and easy and simple. Before he could stop her, she dashed to the tree and found a foothold in the rough bark. She reached up and grabbed a thick branch, her muscles remembering what it once felt like.

Fred rushed over to her, his arms out as if he was afraid she would fall and he would be there to catch her. 'It could be quite dangerous.'

'Not as dangerous as riding into battle as you did, Fred,' she said. Her heart ached to think of him in such danger and she knew she had to try and be brave as he was. He was there with her and that made her feel confident. Certain. She kept pulling herself upwards.

She felt a touch on her leg, through her skirt, and glanced down to see he stood ready to catch her at a moment's notice. She smiled at him, sure she was brave now. He made her so. She kept going, higher and higher, until she found a lovely little spray of leaves. She snapped it off and dropped it to the ground, intending to keep it as a souvenir of this moment.

As she clambered back down, the toe of her half-boot caught in her hem and she felt herself tumbling backward with an instant of cold panic.

But Fred was there, always, to catch her. He held her against him, safe above the hard ground. She held onto his shoulders, feeling the hardness of him through his coat. She felt so very warm and breathless now. Safe.

'Th-thank you, Fred,' she whispered. 'It seems you have saved me again.'

'I'm always here if you need me, remember, Ella?' he said. He held her steady as she found her footing, but she noticed he winced as if his arm worried him.

'You're hurt,' she cried. 'Let me see…'

He laughed and flexed his arm again. 'Not at all. Parfit knights are never hurt when they catch their fair ladies, are they? It's merely a twinge.'

Eleanor wasn't sure she believed him, but she wouldn't embarrass him for the world. She nodded and they turned away from the tree, joking and laughing together again at last. As Fred waved at Penelope, perched above them on the slope of a hill, Eleanor scooped up her leaves and promised herself she would never forget that moment at all.

Penelope perched on a low, flat boulder between a stand of trees, looking out over the town below. Mary had wandered off to sketch a stream, since they hadn't yet encountered any ruins, and Penelope found herself alone. Fred and Eleanor were just hazy figures in the distance, moving in and out of the shadowed sunlight between the trees.

The sunlight filtering and drifting through the canopy of leaves was warm and delicious, flowing like summertime honey over Penelope's skin, chilled for so long, and she drank it in. She took her bonnet off, dangling it by its ribbons, and turned her face up to the light. She didn't care anything about propriety in that moment. That had ruled her life for too long. She kicked up her half-boots under the hem of her sombre lavender pelisse. How nice it would be to wear *real* colours again! To find a way to live once more.

She closed her eyes and listened to a distant song Mary sang as she sketched. Something about a shepherd and his pretty lass and the twitter of birds. Yes, she was truly alone, as she had been ever since she was widowed. Before that, even. Her first marriage had been over in a flash and her second had often been spent alone in her rooms. Yet this solitude felt so very different from all those long, grey, loveless days. This felt filled with sensation and heat and movement. The world gathering all around her once more. There for her to scoop up if she dared to.

Yet there was still that tiny, icy sliver of loneliness deep inside of her. That whisper of regret and yearning she was never quite rid of.

She opened her eyes and gazed out over the town again. The houses and churches, bridges and elegant crescents, like a scattering of toys. A place of play and

forgetfulness. All those days she had spent nursing husbands so much older than her, the crushing knowledge
of the Earl's debts, never knowing where she could
turn.

She'd imagined living in Bath would help her draw a
line under that old life and move forward. Her jointure
could not stretch to London but a small place in Bath
was possible. A place where she could slowly join the
flow of humanity again. Tiptoe into theatres and parties once more, make some friends, go for drives, have
tea. She hadn't quite realised what a marriage mart
Bath was! For people of all ages and situations. It was
as if being surrounded by reminders of one's health all
over, in the waters and doctors' offices, made everyone long to live.

Penelope swung her feet, wondering idly where
among those toy houses she could find a real place for
herself, which was what she longed for most. To decide
who *she* was at long last.

She glimpsed Mary skipping along the river pathway, her sketchbook in one hand and hat in the other,
singing. So young. So filled with spirit! When had Penelope ever felt young? She could barely remember it at
all. Yet once, before she had to marry, there *had* been a
few days. Some parties, friends, laughter and teasing…

And there had been that one moment. Yes, before she
married, before all her responsibility crashed down on
her, when she'd been allowed to attend a house party at
the house of distant cousins. For a brief fortnight, she'd
just been a young lady. Playing croquet on the lawn,

taking tea, charades after dinner, dancing and playing hide-and-seek in the attics.

There had been some young men, too, who wanted to joke and tease and dance with her. Who seemed to find her pretty and interesting. One in particular, maybe? Yes, indeed. Anthony Oliver, a man whose family had made fortunes in mercantile business and were on the edge of gentry. A young man of beautiful dark eyes and an enticing laugh, one who talked with her as if she actually had something to say and danced with her so gracefully. She'd never quite forgotten him.

But that was all. She had to marry soon after. Her father's debts, just like the Earl's, threatening to take away everything. And she, a lady with so few choices, had to save them. No more Anthony Oliver. That party was just a moment. A memory of bright joy.

She turned and glimpsed Fred and Eleanor walking down the pathway, so close to each other. Fred had been a good friend to her when she lived practically alone at Moulton Magna, though he couldn't be there very often. He wrote her letters from his Army postings. Amusing messages that carried her out of her small world and gave her tiny nuggets of advice and of hope. Now he had so many burdens of his own—his injuries, memories of war, restoring his estate. She longed so much to help him now, as he had once helped her. To find him a suitable wife to share his troubles. To shore up Moulton Magna for the future.

She'd heard such good reports of the work of the agency and Eleanor and Mary's family still had a fine reputation in the neighbourhood of Moulton Magna. Surely if anyone could help Fred, it was them.

Now, as she watched the two of them together, wrapped up in each other as if nothing else existed, she felt a touch of hope, just like that sunlight. Yet there was always that grey sense of disquiet. Eleanor St Aubin was the kindest of ladies, but she had no fortune. It was terribly sad, so sad that anyone so good as Fred should be left with such troubles.

Yet he *did* look happy now. Peaceful, as she had not seen him in so long. Surely estates, like people, needed more than money and titles to guard them against the rocks of the world? Surely affection and spirit could carry a great deal?

So the young Penelope had once hoped, but not for long.

She sighed and pushed herself reluctantly to her feet. She shook out her skirts, those drab folds of half-mourning, and turned towards the pathway to join Mary. They did all have to confront the real world again, but not just yet.

She stood, brushing down her skirts before she turned back towards their picnic spot in the distance. At the turning of the path, slanting down towards the stream, she heard a burst of laughter just beyond the curve. It was childish laughter, a shriek, and it made her smile. She swung her hat by its ribbons and prepared to wave at whoever it was and then hurry past.

As she came around the corner, she saw a gentleman and two little girls on the mossy path. The man wore no hat and his glossy dark hair shone in the sunlight.

'Oh!' one of the girls cried. 'What a pretty lady! Is she a forest spirit?'

Penelope, caught off guard, laughed.

'Natalie,' the man admonished. 'Remember manners, yes? Your mama would be very disappointed.'

'Not at all,' Penelope answered. 'Miss Natalie has quite brightened my day! I do think…'

She glanced up at the man—and gasped in shock. *Surely not*. The sun must have stunned her, pushed her back to those old, half-lost memories. That house party, those days of rare freedom and fun. It surely could not be *him*. Anthony Oliver.

For a long moment, they stared at each other in astonishment, as if they faced off over a games table and waited for one to make a move.

'Miss Preston,' he said, his voice as full of shock as she felt, and she knew it really, truly was him. Maybe thoughts and memories had magical powers in that beautiful place. Memories of youthful dances and laughter and the one moment in her life she'd felt free. His dark eyes were the same now as they had been then.

'I am Lady Fleetwood now. But yes, I was Miss Preston,' she said. 'A very long time ago.'

He smiled and those eyes sparkled. How delicious he smelled, too. Warm and woodsy and sweet. And young. So young. 'Not so very long ago as all that. Seeing you, I would vow it was yesterday. I remember that party so well.'

'As do I—Mr Oliver.' Yet in truth, it *had* been a long time since that party and she wondered what he did now. She glanced down at the two adorable little girls, all pink cheeks and dark curls, wide, curious hazel eyes. Her heart gave a sharp pang. 'Are these your darling daughters?' For surely he had a wife and a large family by now, all handsome and boisterous.

He laughed. 'Fortunately, no, for they are imps of mischief in disguise. They are my nieces, my sister's children. Natalie and Grace.'

Grace gave a wobbly curtsy and tried to pop her hand in her mouth, but Natalie grabbed the grubby digits and tugged.

'How do you do,' Natalie said. 'And, Uncle Anthony, Mama says you must not call us *imps* again! You encourage us too much, remember? You especially shouldn't say it in front of fine ladies.' She gave Penelope a beaming smile. 'Uncle Anthony is usually most proper, I promise.'

Penelope laughed even harder. They were adorable—and they were not his! 'Yet I recall a time he was not so very well-mannered…'

'Oh, please! Lady Fleetwood, no tales of my misspent youth to get back to their mother. She fusses at me enough as it is.' He smiled at her, a delighted grin, and the heart she'd been determined to close off so long ago cracked open again. 'It is very nice to see you again. I often wondered after that party how you fared.'

He had thought of her? As she had him? 'Did you indeed, Mr Oliver?'

'Yes. Do you and your—your husband reside here in Bath?'

'I do live here now, yes. I fear Lord Fleetwood is no longer with us.'

His smile dimmed and he nodded in sad understanding. 'I am sorry for your loss.'

'How kind. Tell me, have you and your—your wife been in town long?'

The two girls watched them avidly, their wide gazes swinging between them.

'I am not married, sadly,' he said. 'I am visiting my sister and her family.'

'He has *never* been married,' Natalie offered. 'Mama says there is no lady to suit him, though she tries to find one.'

Poor Anthony's face turned quite crimson and Penelope had to stifle another laugh. She longed to burst into giggles. To fall over with mirth! She hadn't felt quite so young and giddy in—well, ever since that long-ago house party.

She glimpsed Mary strolling up the path towards them. 'I believe I know someone who could help you with that…'

'Our mama would be *ever* so grateful if you could, Lady Fleetwood,' Natalie said primly, like a dowager gossiping over tea. 'Grace and I require cousins.'

Grace nodded emphatically.

Penelope studied Anthony, that gorgeous face of his, and couldn't help but picture *his* children. They would be lovely. 'I shall make the introduction, then.'

'Perhaps I could call on you to obtain this pertinent information?' he asked, shuffling his feet in a strangely hopeful manner. She did see those long-ago days in his eyes—the moments of being young and free and laughing. 'And renew our old acquaintance.'

Penelope felt a bolt of pure, warm pleasure at the thought of seeing him again. 'Certainly, Mr Oliver.' She un-looped her reticule from her wrist and took out a card to pass him, with her address, wondering if she was being foolish. He bowed, promising to call soon, and left again with the two skipping, giggling girls.

Penelope feared she, too, had a silly, schoolgirlish smile on her face and she wasn't entirely sure why. Or maybe she just didn't want to *admit* why. That she wanted to see this man again too much.

She dared to glance back over her shoulder at Mr Oliver's retreating figure. She hoped Mary hadn't seen the meeting. That she could hold it to herself like a delicious little secret for just a little while longer, but of course that was too much to hope.

Mary looked curious indeed when she reached Penelope, her eyes wide and shining under the frill of her bonnet. 'Who was *that*, Penelope? I haven't seen him around Bath before.'

Penelope laughed. 'And you know *everyone* in Bath?'

'Of course. It is my job to know them. And I'm quite sure I'd remember a face like that!'

Penelope pushed down a silly, jealous little pang. 'He is rather handsome, I admit.'

Mary tilted her head as she studied Penelope, who hoped her feelings didn't show too clearly. 'You are acquainted with him?'

'Somewhat. His name is Mr Anthony Oliver. We met at a house party, many years ago, before I married. He was—most amiable.'

Mary's head tilted even further. 'Indeed?' She looped her arm through Penelope's and they strolled along the path again, quite as if the world hadn't shaken around her. 'Tell me, will you and Fred be at the assembly rooms tomorrow evening? It's always a terrible crush, of course, but the dancing is usually of fine quality. Everyone can be seen there.'

Penelope smiled down at Mary. She was rather like Penelope had once been, in her younger, more optimistic days. 'Everyone you know.'

'Knowing people is my bread and butter. And it's a great deal of fun! I didn't know your Mr Oliver, though. I wonder if he will be at the assembly. If so, then you *must* come.'

Penelope thought over this, imagining dancing with Anthony as she had so long ago and almost giggled with a burst of excitement. 'Why?'

Mary twirled around. 'To dance with him, of course! Even from a distance I could see he admired you.'

'I fear my dancing days may be over.'

'What nonsense! You are in the very prime of dancing life, Pen.' They paused to watch Eleanor and Fred coming towards them, dappled in the sunlight as they laughed together. 'Do you think Fred could also be persuaded to come to the assembly? Or does he think his dancing days are past, too?'

Penelope studied Mary's expression beneath her straw, frilled bonnet. Mary looked like a china shepherdess, all blonde curls and pink cheeks, yet Penelope was certainly learning never to underestimate either of the St Aubin sisters. 'He might think that. He has born

so many burdens of late. But I am of the firm opinion
he is wrong and he must be persuaded of that. He must
enjoy life again for a while.'

'I definitely agree. We must make sure you are *both*
at the assembly. And that he mingles in the ballroom,
not just disappearing into the card room.'

'You have a candidate—a lady in mind for him?'

'Perhaps. I must consult with Eleanor and Harry and
hear their thoughts on the possibility.'

Penelope nodded, watching as Fred and Eleanor
laughed again, their heads bent close together, as if
they had always been just like that. Penelope saw the
old Fred just then. The laughing young man who had
welcomed her into his home and been her friend. The
man who hadn't yet been stricken with pain and burdens. He looked…

He looked happy.

Penelope glanced at Mary to see if she saw it, too.
That connection between Fred and Eleanor. Mary just
watched, expressionless.

Penelope suddenly ached for Fred, as she once had
for herself. A heart, no matter how well-guarded one
thought it was, was a frail, vulnerable thing and she
didn't want Fred to be hurt any more than he already
had. Hurt by a love that couldn't be.

But if he truly loved Eleanor…

'Can you not give me some hint of who the lady
might be?' Penelope asked.

Mary shook her head. 'We shall all know soon
enough. Just come to the assembly and meet some
people. It will be a pleasant diversion, if nothing else.'

Penelope sighed. They continued their walk, sunlight and shadow falling over them. 'I should certainly welcome a diversion, I declare.'

Chapter Seven

Eleanor St Aubin was a most unusual lady indeed. Fred had always known that. Her care and empathy for others had made her treasured in her father's parish and she had laughter like a sunny day. But now she'd grown even more into herself. Warm and caring, with her soft smile and magical laughter, she drew Fred closer and closer every time he saw her. She made his world a brighter place at long last.

He carefully studied himself in the looking glass as he painstakingly tied his cravat for the assembly. His scars seemed to have faded there in Bath, looking like mere pale streaks against his skin and he was as strong and fit as ever now that his strength had returned. Surely he was not *too* ruined for the ordinary joys of life now, for holding a lady's hand, laughing with her—kissing her.

Yet he knew very well the truth. There was really no use for such wishful thinking, for trying to remake the world. He was too old now. He felt so very much older than the Fred who was once Eleanor's friend at Moulton Magna. He was too changed by his years at war. Too weighed down by responsibility to think about a sweet lady like Eleanor. She was too kind to deserve his troubles—his crumbling estate, his nightmares from the war, the distrust it all left in his heart—and too caught in responsibility to family, just as he was. They wouldn't be good for one another. Not situated as they both were in life.

Yet the pleasure he felt when he thought of her, when he could actually be in the warmth of her presence, was there and there was no mistaking it. When she was near, it was as if the sun shone all the time. He longed to know what was behind those unfathomable eyes of hers and that little smile as she watched the world around her. Despite what she had been dealt in life, there was always that spark of humour, of delight in people, and in music, and in nature and in poetry, which made him delight in it all again, too.

Her sweetness was always unchanged, as was his craving for it.

Fred shook his head as he studied that slightly crooked cravat. Like himself, the lack of perfection and symmetry, couldn't quite be worthy of Eleanor. Yet it was all he had. He fastened it with a cameo-headed pin and smoothed his hair. He had no place for someone like her in his life now, nor she for him. When he went into the Army, he left his wild days behind him. He'd vowed he would change. That he would be a man his family and home could rely on. That he could be worthy of someone like Eleanor. But to be that he had to be apart from her.

He glanced out through the window at the gathering evening, purple-blue and shimmering. Surely, though, trying to be responsible and noble didn't mean he couldn't have the rare, golden pleasure of a dance with Eleanor on such a night…

Eleanor peeked curiously out of the window of their hansom as they joined the long line of vehicles and pedestrians snaking their way towards the assembly rooms, as they did every week. She'd been there many times before, of course. Meeting potential matches, playing cards, sipping wine, listening to valuable gossip—it was all an important part of her job.

Tonight, though, she felt quite unaccountably excited about it all. Nervous. She twisted her fan between her gloved fingers as she looked around, seeing things familiar yet new. She had barely been able to sleep last night, or concentrate on her work that day, for thinking about Fred there in the sunlight and Fred holding her hand. His smile, the touch of his lips on her skin, the sparkle of everything around him. Would she see him that night? She did long for that. And also dreaded it.

The familiar building, with its pillared portico, looked transformed in the evening. Golden light spilled from every window and doorway, a bright diamond shimmer in the purple-black night. Laughter rang out from the revellers making their way to front doors, with feathers waving merrily and jewels sparkling.

'Oh, look, Eleanor, there are Miss Evans and her mother,' Mary whispered, the ribbons in her hair nodding as she smiled at their newest patrons. 'Miss Evans *is* pretty, I think, even if she is terribly quiet. Who

could blame her, with such a mother! I do think she
would do well for Fred, don't you? That lovely dowry!'

Eleanor studied Miss Evans for a moment, trying
to compose how to answer. She and Mary had spoken
of Miss Evans, along with one or two other potential
matches, and Eleanor had been a bit surprised by the
notion. Surprised and, yes, discomfited, if she had to
admit it to herself. Even if she knew in her head that
Fred needed such a wife, her heart refused to quite cooperate yet.

On a professional level, Eleanor couldn't disagree
with Mary. From an agency point of view, it could be
a fine match. But her heart felt torn in two to put all
her feelings aside and admit this, to be sensible again.
'Perhaps you are right, Mary. But shouldn't they meet
first, before we decide she must be the one?'

'Of course I am right!' Mary declared. 'And they
will meet, I'm sure, perhaps even this very evening.
And speaking of matches, did you perchance see Penelope's old friend Mr Oliver on our walk on Beechen
Cliff yesterday?'

Eleanor thought back and recalled glimpsing Penelope chatting with a man in a handsomely tailored blue
coat, along with two little girls. Penelope had seemed
most absorbed in the conversation, even from that distance, and she had not spoken of it after. 'The one with
the two children? So he knew Penelope?'

'Indeed. All she would really say is they met at a
house party before she was married, but I could see
there must be much more. Such longing between them!
So I did a bit of research.'

'In a day? How efficient of you, Mary.' But Eleanor wasn't really surprised. Mary was usually very efficient indeed, as well as being a romantic at heart. She had a sharp instinct for what would, or could, work. So if Mary saw something in Penelope and this Mr Oliver, she probably wasn't wrong. Though she was wrong about Miss Evans.

'Of course. Pen deserves someone truly worthy, doesn't she? Someone to win her heart and make her happy. After old Lord Fleetwood and his troubles...'

Troubles that had now landed on Fred. The estate and all its tenants and workers. The crumbling house that meant he had to marry an heiress. 'And what did you find?'

'Mr Oliver is quite well-off indeed, though he is self-made. He owns several business concerns, built up from his family's textile imports concern, and he just bought a fine house in Surrey. He has never been married. Too busy working, I'm sure, which means he needs a wife to manage his household and help him in society. He is also wonderfully handsome! I'm quite sure he fell deeply in love with Pen all those years ago and never married as no lady could compare to her.' Mary sighed happily at the thought.

Eleanor laughed. 'You should write novels! I agree Penelope deserves a happy match, but I fear neither of them are patrons of the agency. How can we help?'

Mary waved this away with a flick of her lace fan. 'We can surely assist a friend! I shall think of something. Oh, look, there is Lady Banks! Good heavens, what a turban, have you ever seen such colours? Would it look well on me? I shall have to find out her milliner…'

Eleanor smiled as she watched her sister vanish into the crowd. She took a glass of wine and found a quieter corner near the fireplace where she could examine the scene. The people finding their dance partners with shy smiles, the husbands slipping off to the card room, the friends calling greetings. This was one of the reasons she enjoyed Bath life and enjoyed her work. Helping people to find happiness and to enjoy their lives as much as possible in such congenial surroundings was a dream to her.

And suddenly, appearing in a gap in the crowd, was Fred himself, arm in arm with Penelope. He was smiling at something Pen said to him, his face alight and so young in that moment, the harsh lines of worry and pain erased. He had a new coat. A dark green superfine fitted perfectly over his broad, strong shoulders, the stark white of his cravat framing his square, chiselled jaw. A wave of amber-gold hair swept over his brow and he flicked it back.

In the glow of the candles, his scars could barely be seen and several ladies turned their heads to watch him walk past with avid interest. Surely they only saw his heroic, dashing *mien*. Penelope was soon claimed for a dance, and to Eleanor's surprise, instead of asking one of the young ladies to partner him, Fred came to her side, a smile on his lips that made her smile in return.

A rush of latecomers poured through the doors, racing to claim their partners for the next set and find places in the lines forming on the parquet floor beneath the sparkle of the chandeliers. The whole night had taken on a diamond-bright shimmer.

'Shall we join them, Eleanor?' Fred asked, gesturing to the dancers. She peeked up at him, to see he smiled at her ruefully, crookedly, a tiny flash of white that made her heart stutter. Was he really offering to open the dancing with her, to give her the first dance of the evening? 'My dancing skills have never been of the finest, but I'm sure I can manage not to quite disgrace myself.'

Eleanor laughed, put entirely at her ease with him again, as was always the way with Fred. He made her feel discomfited, fidgety. But then there was that wonderful feeling of ease and knowing. Of being with someone she knew. Or once thought she knew. 'It's been a long time since I did more than observe the dancing, but perhaps if we just follow the others we could muddle along.'

Fred offered her his arm and she slipped her gloved hand lightly over his sleeve, as she had many times before. But at this moment it all felt new. His arm felt so warm and strong under her touch, holding her steady as he led her into the crowd. Those ladies still watched him, whispering behind their fans.

She glanced up at Fred, wondering if he noticed them and he smiled back at her. The candlelight, the music and laughter, the scent of roses and perfume and wine. And, above all, the feeling of Fred beside her again after so long. Real and not a dream. Not a memory. Surely it was something, one small moment, she could savour? It couldn't last long, she knew that, but it was a wonderful, sparkling feeling all the same.

She longed to forget the agency, forget being sensible and responsible, just for one dance. She gave him a quick, delighted smile and vowed she *would* forget it all for this moment. She would just think of him.

They found their places at the end of the dance. In Bath, such gatherings always seemed meant for younger ladies than Eleanor—ladies who were fresh and innocent, seeking their futures, while hers had slipped beyond her before she even realised it. But now she felt truly a part of it all. Part of the fun and laughter and excitement of the dance.

The lead couple stepped off, skipping together then apart, twirling behind the next pair and everyone else in the line followed. Eleanor found her feet remembered the steps. Skipping right then left, turning, spinning and coming back to find Fred's hand again. How light she felt—as if she could float right out of her slippers! The music wound around her, carrying her forward. She couldn't help but laugh as Fred touched her hand, his fingers sliding over hers, and they cast off and around, meeting again. Their feet flew together, back and forth, light as whipped cream as she swirled around him. It was as if they'd always moved together just that way.

The lavish, glittering room with its pastel walls and domed ceiling, the jewels and silks and laces, all blurred together dizzily as Fred caught her arm in a turn. His bad arm was tucked behind his back, barely to be seen.

He stumbled a bit and Eleanor smiled as they righted themselves together and danced on, perfectly matched in their movements, bearing each other ever forward.

'I did say I was never much of a dancer, didn't I?' he said, his voice full of wonderful laughter. He turned them faster and faster as the music grew, until she giggled.

She, sensible Eleanor St Aubin, *giggling*! It was a magical, topsy-turvy night indeed.

'You do give yourself far too little credit, Fred,' she said. 'You have always been a splendid dancer indeed!'

'I am too out of practice,' he said.

He did not feel 'out of practice' one jot as his arm slipped around her waist for another turn. Eleanor felt so delicate in his arms, a true fairy queen born above the world by her knight.

They spun once more and the music, which had been winding higher and higher around them, crashed down in a great finale. Eleanor skidded to a halt, still holding on to Fred as she tried to catch her breath, tried to float down to earth once more. The blur around her slowed and turned solid again, other dancers bowing and curtsying, the chandelier going still above her head.

He bowed low to her and she curtsied in answer, trying to catch her breath. She didn't want to part from him, not yet. If only her moment could go on and on…

'Shall we take a stroll? Perhaps seek out some refreshments?' Fred asked. He sounded eager, even a bit unsure, as if he too didn't want the dance to end just yet. 'You can tell me more about Bath society and the people around us. Pen says I cannot go on being a grumpy old hermit.'

'I don't think you are grumpy and not *terribly* old,' Eleanor teased as they made their way to the quieter edge of the room. 'But if you want to find a wife, society is a necessity.'

Eleanor glimpsed Miss Evans near the doors to the card room, looking very young and pretty in a new, very stylish, pink-striped silk gown. Her mother was nowhere in sight for the moment. Miss Evans was speaking with a tall, slim, dark-haired, poetically pale young man Eleanor recognised as Mr Overbury, a young curate whose older sister had recently met her fiancé through the agency. He was handsome, true and beautifully musical, but not of great fortune. Surely Mrs Evans would not be happy her daughter was spending time with a 'mere' curate! Especially if she knew an earl was nearby...

'You see that young lady in pink just over there, by the card room?' Eleanor said.

'The one with the silver feathers in her hair?'

'Indeed. Now, you must not breathe a word that I spoke to you of any agency business, but her name is Pamela Evans and she and her mother paid us a visit in recent days. Her father has accrued a great fortune in industry and they wish for her to marry well. Mary thinks she might be a possible match for you.' She forced away that touch of cold reluctance and made herself smile.

Fred's eyes narrowed as he studied Miss Evans. 'For me?'

'Yes. I think her mother would be very impressed by a fine old title.'

'And what does the lady seek?' he asked quietly, still studying Miss Evans as she laughed with Mr Overbury.

Eleanor frowned in thought as she watched the young lady and the curate. It was rather hard to decipher what Miss Evans might want for herself as she was so quiet. So unreadable. Eleanor knew she or Mary would have to find a way to speak to her alone soon. 'To own the truth, I am not quite sure. She is a quiet lady and who could blame her when her mother loves to talk so much. She is very pretty.'

'And what of you, Eleanor?'

'Me?' she said, confused. 'I am not so pretty…'

He laughed. 'I do beg to differ on that. But I meant, Mary thinks Miss Evans would make a fine Lady Fleetwood. What do you think of that?'

Eleanor thought no lady would be worthy of being Lady Fleetwood now, not really. But he must marry. It was the way of the world. She had always known that. But she hadn't realised how much it would hurt to face those facts herself one day. To do what she must do. But she cared about Fred far too much to not help him. 'I think…'

They were jostled a bit by the growing crowd and someone stepped on Eleanor's hem making her gasp. 'Shall we walk outside a bit on the terrace I saw earlier?' Fred said. 'Get a bit of air.'

'Yes, I'd like that,' she answered, though she knew she shouldn't be alone with Fred like that. It was simply too tempting, the soft night air beckoning her with a gentle breeze.

They were alone for the moment under the starry

sky, only a few couples in the distance, and they strolled between the potted trees in silence. Eleanor studied him there in the shadows and a thousand things passed through her mind. Things she longed to say that she never could. That he should forget the Miss Evans of the world. That she, Eleanor, was right there! Yet she wasn't there, not really. She could only take the bits of his presence she could have now, while she still could.

'Have you never thought of using your agency to find your own match, Ella?' he asked as they stopped near the balustrade, staring out into the night.

Surprised by the question, she quickly shook her head. 'I couldn't do that! It's only a business, really, and no one I have met there would suit me anyway. I sometimes do wonder if it might not be good for Mary, though…'

Fred laughed softly. 'You St Aubin girls. Like the most attractive nettles, blossoms hiding prickles. In a sweet way, of course. It would be hard to get so close to you.'

She turned towards him, studying him in the moonlight. Yes, in some ways he had changed from the young man who had been her friend. But in some ways he was, he felt, just the same. She reached up and lightly traced the chiselled line of his jaw with her gloved fingertips, feeling a muscle tense beneath her touch. 'Yet you have always been close to me.'

They'd known each other so long, denied themselves so long. Danced away and around and beyond. She'd told herself it had to be that way and surely he had, too. But just now, none of that mattered. All that mattered was the raw longing that washed over her. All she could see was him, all she knew was him. She couldn't stay away now.

'And you to me, Ella.' His hands circled her waist, tugging her closer. She went, unresisting, curious, filled with the need to be close to him. It was dizzying and she clutched at his shoulders to hold herself upright. All her senses tipped and whirled and she knew only him.

As if in a hazy dream, far away but more real and immediate than anything she'd ever known before, his head bent towards hers and he kissed her.

The touch of his lips was soft at first. Velvety, warm, pressing teasingly once, twice. When she did not, *could* not, move away, instead she leaned closer to him and his kiss deepened. Became hotter, more urgent, answering her own need.

The world utterly vanished and there was only him. Only that one perfect moment. And she longed to seize it completely. Remember it for ever.

Yet it was a moment that shattered all too soon. A shout from the street below broke into her dream, dragging her back down to earth with a hard thud, reminding her where she was, who she was and what she risked there. Her reputation. Her heart.

She tore her mouth from his, tipping back her head to suck in a deep breath of night air.

'Ella,' he said hoarsely, stepping away from her. 'Ella, I—I cannot…'

'No,' she managed to whisper. Her heart and mind were in a jumble and she couldn't think at all. She longed for him, but he could not be hers. Never be hers.

Not really. She was losing herself. Losing him. 'Please don't say you're sorry.'

'How could I be sorry? But I must say…'

Eleanor shook her head fiercely. She couldn't speak. Couldn't think. Couldn't make sense of this moment. Not yet. Not when he was so close to her. 'I must go!' she gasped and ran away, leaving him there in the perfect night.

Just a bit earlier that evening...

Mary studied the cards in her hand, just as she studied the room around her, taking in every detail in one discreet, sweeping glance.

She especially studied the others at her table. Lord Coulton, a young poet who kept beseeching the agency to help him in his quest to find an artistic soulmate, a true muse, while also trying in vain to court Mary herself, she could dismiss for the moment. It was Penelope and Mr Oliver who held her attention.

Penelope had declared he was only someone she met once, long ago, at a house party. But Mary was certain there was more—far more—to the tale. Her matchmaking nose was itching.

'Have you resided long in Bath, Miss St Aubin?' Mr Oliver asked as he laid down a card.

'For some time, yes. My father was vicar at Moulton Magna village and when he sadly passed away my sister and I came here.'

'Her father was a veritable angel and so well-read. He knew all the philosophers and theologians and gave the most engaging sermons,' Penelope said. 'We were bereft to lose such a fine family, so I am happy to have the St Aubin sisters as neighbours again.' She glanced at Mr Oliver from under her lashes, a small smile hovering over her lips. 'It is such a pleasure to find old friends again, is it not?'

He smiled at her in return and, for an instant, Mary was sure they saw no one else at all.

'And how do you enjoy town life, Miss St Aubin?' he asked, studying his cards again.

'Very much!' Mary enthused. 'I love the assemblies and concerts. Sometimes I wonder what London must be like, with even more theatres and pleasure gardens.'

'Have you often visited London?' Mr Overbury said eagerly. 'I should love to show it to you…'

'How sweet of you, Mr Overbury! But when we find your muse at last, you shall want only to show *her* the sites,' Mary said, patting his hand. 'I fear I have only visited London once, when I was quite young and most overwhelmed by it all. I visited the Tower and Westminster Abbey and various other churches my father insisted on. I long to go back and see more. To see everything!'

'Perhaps you will fall in love with a London gentleman and be whisked away as his wife to a mansion in Berkeley Square!' Penelope teased. 'With so many visitors to Bath, who knows who we might meet?'

Mary laughed. The thought of marriage for *herself* always seemed such an odd and unthinkable thing. Her schemes were always for patrons. Her joy came from fitting them together like puzzle pieces and then seeing their happiness. She enjoyed making matches too much to become one herself.

Penelope, on the other hand…

She studied Penelope and Mr Oliver again as they murmured over their cards, their hands brushing. At the touch, Pen's cheeks went quite rosy, which Mary found fascinating.

Yes, a match for Penelope would be most satisfying. And one for Eleanor, though Mary wouldn't say so to her sister. Mary did often wish that dearest Eleanor would meet a man truly worthy of her and be swept off to a lovely life with a home and children, after all her hard work taking care of Papa and Mary herself for so long. She remembered seeing Eleanor walking with Fred along Beechen Cliff, their heads bent together, fitting together so perfectly.

Why did it have to be Fred, now?

Mary sighed. It was much too sad that Eleanor and Fred could not be, that Fred's duty took him away from them. Yet surely there was *someone* out there who would be just right. Who would be truly worthy of her sister. She glanced around the card tables, evaluating the gentlemen she saw there. Too old, too young, too flighty, too serious.

And too clergyish, she thought as she glimpsed that handsome young Mr Overbury strolling near the refreshment tables. No matter how lovely, Eleanor did not deserve to be a vicarage servant again. And Mr Overbury…

He seemed very absorbed by the lady who walked beside him, arm in arm. And that lady was Miss Evans.

'Mary?' Penelope said, studying the fallen cards before them. 'Are you well?'

Mary made herself laugh. 'Oh, yes, you were asking about marriage! Well, I have no desire to wed, at least not yet. I enjoy my life too much to change.'

'Mary has been telling me about a masquerade ball to be held at Sydney Gardens,' Penelope said. 'It should be most exciting! Costumes, music. Shall you be there, Mr Oliver?'

He smiled at her, wide and wondering, setting off Mary's matchmaking senses once more. 'If you will be there, Lady Fleetwood, I should enjoy it very much.'

'We should take a box,' Mary said. And she would be sure Penelope and Mr Oliver sat right next to each other.

'Anthony? By Jove it *is* you,' a deep, chocolate-rich voice, lightly touched with a Scots burr, said. The sound made prickles unaccountably tingle at the back of Mary's neck, like a fine opera aria could do. She shivered and longed to hear that voice again.

'Campbell!' Mr Oliver said, leaping to his feet to hold out his hand to the gentleman who approached them. 'How splendid to see you. When did you arrive in Bath? I heard nothing of your coming here.'

Mary glanced up and gasped when she saw the most extraordinary gentleman standing there. Very tall, broad-shouldered, with too-long, auburn-streaked dark hair falling over his brow just above bright green eyes. He wore the most fashionable, conventional evening coat of dark blue, with a cream waistcoat and well-tied cravat. But he might as well have been wearing a kilt as he strode over hills, a broadsword in hand.

Suddenly overcome with a ridiculous confusion and a warm flush spreading over her cheeks and throat as if she had been in the sun too long, Mary stared down hard at the new cards in her hand.

'Only this week. Adele declared she was in great need of society and I could not spare the time for London, so I thought to give her a little treat for a few days,' Mr Campbell answered, his emerald gaze sweeping over the table. It caught and lingered on Mary, a small frown on his lips as if he sought to read her thoughts.

Mary made herself smile back, carelessly, brightly. *Adele.* Was that his wife? For surely such a man must be married. The name 'Adele' made her sound like a dainty, china-doll-pretty creature. The two of them together would look like a pair from a novel.

'Bath is a fine choice, I'm sure.' Mr Oliver turned to indicate the others at the table. 'Lady Fleetwood, Miss St Aubin, Lord Coulton, may I present a cousin of mine, Charles Campbell? He lives in Scotland most of the time and I haven't seen him in some time. He's also been much occupied as guardian to our young kinswoman, Adele. Charles, this is Lady Fleetwood, who I once met when we were impossibly young. And Miss St Aubin, who is a resident of this fair town, as is Lord Coulton, a fine poet.'

'How do you do?' Mr Campbell said with a small bow. 'Miss St Aubin…'

'We are just finishing our hand, Mr Campbell and I fear I have lost most shockingly,' Mary said, hoping she sounded light and unaffected by this man's touch. By his night-dark eyes. By the intense way he looked at her. 'Will you take my place? I should go find my sister.'

'I would enjoy that, thank you, Miss St Aubin,' he said, his gaze never leaving her until she feared she would drop the cards in a flustered flurry again.

'Charles was a terrible sharper in our misspent youth,' Mr Oliver declared. 'We all constantly owed him our pocket money!'

'Anthony, you shall misrepresent me to these fine ladies,' Charles Campbell protested, though he laughed, a rough, low, rumbling sound Mary was sure she could feel all the way to her toes. 'I merely had more patience to practise than you. But I fear I must now decline and play with you on another evening. I left Adele dancing.'

'Mr Campbell!' Penelope cried. 'I am sure you shouldn't have left her alone in such a crush.'

Mr Campbell shifted on his feet, a look of chagrin on his dark, chiselled face that made Mary want to reassure him. Comfort him. Help him.

Oh, she was in trouble.

'You see what a terrible inadequate chaperon I am?' he said. 'I feel I am constantly learning new duties, new pitfalls.'

Penelope laughed, but Mary thought Mr Campbell looked so genuinely baffled she couldn't help but give him a reassuring smile as she folded up her cards. 'Dance sets do tend to be long here at the assembly rooms and Mr Derrick, the Master of Ceremonies, keeps a sharp eye on the proceedings at all times. I'm sure there is a very small scope for mischief, even if the young lady was determined.'

He gave her a little bow, a little, secret smile on his lips. 'I dare say you had much determination, Miss St Aubin.'

Mary tilted her head as she examined him, wondering if he teased her, criticised—maybe even admired? He was a wonderful puzzlement. 'I might have, once. Now I am an old spinster and can be a most devoted chaperon when needed. Shall I walk with you to find Miss Adele? I should look for my sister, anyway.'

'That would be most appreciated, thank you, Miss St Aubin.' Mr Campbell gave her a gallant bow. 'Anthony, shall I call on you this week?'

'Certainly. You owe me a chance to win my pride back at the card table.'

'I fear I am truly a poor chaperon—a poor guardian altogether,' Mr Campbell said ruefully as he and Mary made their way through the crowded room. She knew she should pay attention to what was around her, check with patrons, but all she could seem to focus on was *him*. Most extraordinary. 'I've always lived alone you see, Miss St Aubin, and I've become too set in my ways.'

He'd never married at all? Mary found that hard to believe. Surely every lady within a hundred miles had yearned after him! Yet there was certain satisfaction there, too. Not for herself, she told herself sternly, although not quite convincingly. But because he must have high standards. Maybe he wished to marry only for great love! So romantic. 'How old is Miss Adele?'

'Just now seventeen. Her parents, my distant cousins, sadly died from a fever a year ago and I became her guardian. I'm trying to bring her out in society. To give her a place in the world and help her be happy but…' He held out his hand in a helpless gesture and Mary's heart ached for him.

'I am sure she is very fortunate to have you. It is not an easy age for a young lady, especially one who has lost her parents,' she said.

'She seems more cheerful since we came to Bath. She smiles more and is more interested in what is happening around her, which gives me hope.' A tiny frown appeared on his brow as he looked at the crowd around them. 'But I fear I am ill-equipped to help her find something—well, more serious. She has a fortune, you see. Not the largest. But it could be of definite interest to more—unscrupulous elements. And she is pretty, of a trusting nature. She deserves so much happiness in life.'

'Then she is doubly lucky to have a guardian like yourself to watch out for her. Someone who cares for her.' Mary studied the couples strolling past, the knots of young ladies whispering and giggling next to the pastel pink walls. 'Which one is Miss Adele?'

'Just there, in the pale green gown, with the blonde hair,' he said, pride written large in his tone.

Mary turned to examined her. Yes, pretty. Golden hair, like fairy-spun silk, twisted atop a Grecian head and bound with a pearl bandeau. A heart-shaped face with sweet eyes. Not too tall or too short. Slim in fashionable pale green silk. She glanced around shyly but with interest. A small smile on her rosebud lips. Yes, very pretty. And with a fortune *and* a handsome guardian in the bargain. Mary wondered dreamily, hopefully, if one or both of the Campbells could use the agency's services. It would be quite a coup...

The dance set ended and as Mary and Mr Campbell watched, Miss Adele was quickly approached by two eager young gentlemen.

'You need have no fear of Mr Parker,' Mary said, gesturing at the taller of the two. 'I fear you can see his somewhat...misguided choice of waistcoats, but he is most respectable and has a fine estate. The other one—hmm, I am not so sure. Lord Teller has only just arrived in Bath but I would be wary. He is very often a habitue of the racecourses.'

Mr Campbell nodded, looking at her with an impressed tilt of his smile. 'You know much of Bath society then, Miss St Aubin?' he asked.

'Indeed. One might say it is even rather a—career.'

He laughed in delight. 'I should be very interested to hear more, then. Shall we go meet Adele and then perhaps join the next dance set ourselves?'

Mary studied him carefully and finally smiled and nodded. 'Thank you, Mr Campbell. I do enjoy a dance very much indeed...'

Chapter Eight

'After all our time here, Eleanor, I vow I do not know why it must always rain in Bath,' Mary sighed as she gazed out through the window of Molland's confectionery shop. Despite the steady downpour, people hurried past laden with packages, intent on errands, while inside all was warm and creamy with the scents of sugar and spices.

Eleanor studied the scene, too. But she didn't see the shop windows across the street, the bobbing umbrellas scurrying past, or the carriages casting up plumes of water to splash at those umbrellas. Instead her head was filled with visions of the assembly room, dancing with Fred, the stars wheeling overhead as she held onto his arm in the music-echoing night, the touch of his hand…

She shivered.

'Eleanor?' she heard Mary say, the words fizzy and echoing, as if they came from a long distance away. As if she was caught in those dreamlike moments she never wanted to end.

She blinked and glanced across the little round table

at her sister. Mary's face was creased with concern under her feathered bonnet.

'Yes?'

'Are you quite well, Eleanor, dear? You seem so pre-occupied. It's not at all like you.'

Eleanor made herself smile reassuringly. 'I'm quite well, I promise. Just a bit tired. You're right, it's all the rain. But at least we have Molland's marzipan!' She held out the dish of pink and green sweets and Mary popped one in her mouth with a happy sigh. Ever since childhood, Mary could reliably be distracted with confectionery. Miss Muffins, sitting at their feet, looked up with hope on her little face.

'It's no wonder you're weary,' Mary said. 'I am rather tired, myself. So much happening! Assemblies and theatres, and the masquerade to look forward to. I vow I counted at least five possible new patrons for the agency at the assembly rooms.'

'Five?' Eleanor asked sharply, wondering how many of them would be for Fred.

Mary ticked them off on her fingers. 'Lady Hertford and Mrs Miller-Forster, that charming young widow who just moved into the Crescent. Those two will be looking about soon, at least. And I saw Lord and Lady Amson! I am so happy for them. They just married last month and declared their undying gratitude to the agency.'

'Yes, of course. How charming they were together. I was very happy when they matched together.' Eleanor thought with a bittersweet pang of the bliss she'd seen on the newly married couple's faces when last they met. When Lord Amson first came to the agency, she wasn't at all sure who might suit him. But there was someone for everyone. Happiness waiting everywhere.

If only she could find that, too. She would just have to look for her joy in the matches they made, that was all.

'And Penelope and Mr Oliver looked so happy while they played cards together,' Mary went on. 'They could scarcely look away from each other!'

Eleanor laughed. 'Mary! I thought we agreed we should not yet meddle with people who aren't agency patrons.'

'I said they were not *officially* patrons. I did not say I wouldn't meddle just a bit! Penelope is so lovely. She deserves some happiness in life after being married to old Lord Fleetwood. And surely you saw how Mr Oliver watches her. So meltingly gorgeous!'

Eleanor had to agree. When they were in the same room together, Penelope and Anthony Oliver did watch one another when they thought no one was looking. Such longing. It made Eleanor feel so much for them, hope for them. 'But I am sure they don't need our help.'

'Maybe just a tiny push in the right direction, if the chance presents itself. Penelope has grown too accustomed to thinking of others all the time, not herself. She may need assistance in—thinking a different way.'

'Maybe if Penelope asks for our help or advice. Who else did you meet at the assembly that may be looking for a match?'

'A man named Mr Campbell, a cousin of Mr Oliver. Did you meet him?'

'I don't believe so.'

'I was introduced to him while I played cards with Penelope and Mr Oliver. Oh, and with Lord Coulton, we must find him a muse match *soon*, he is becoming so puppyish around me. Anyway, Mr Campbell is a widower with a fine estate and very good-looking indeed. But he is a new guardian to a young lady, Adele Campbell, something of an heiress. And I could see right away how overwhelming it must be for a gentleman on his own to steer a young lady to a suitable match. He surely needs a wife to help him.'

Eleanor glanced sharply at her sister. There was something rather odd, something soft and dreamy, in her sister's voice when she said that name. 'Have you someone in mind for Mr Campbell?'

Mary studied the bit of marzipan in her hand with an odd expression on her face—thoughtful and wistful. 'Not yet. It would have to be someone truly special.'

'We can go over our files as soon as we get home. Any other matches you considered?'

'Miss Evans and Fred, of course! I am still convinced of the possibilities there.'

Eleanor frowned. 'They barely spoke last night, as far as I could see. Miss Evans seemed to enjoy the company of Mr Overbury, that lovely young curate. He really brought her out of her shell when they were dancing.'

Mary waved this away, Miss Muffins avidly watching the bit of marzipan moving in her fingers. 'Her parents would never match her with a curate, I fear. A dance isn't a match, either, Eleanor, you know this.'

Eleanor nodded. She *did* know that. All too well. Just as she knew the sort of wife Fred required.

'Oh, look!' Mary cried. 'The rain has stopped. And is that a bit of sunshine I see? Let's take a stroll by the river, shall we? I am sure Miss Muffins needs to stretch her paws a bit.'

'Of course. A fine idea.' Eleanor could certainly use a breath of fresh air, too. Something to distract her from thinking constantly of Fred. The walk beside the Avon was a lovely one. Lined with trees and roses, and elegant stone bridges leading towards the green hills. Yes, a fine distraction for an hour. She gathered up Miss Muffins's leash and her reticule and watched Mary pop the last of the candy into her mouth with a happy sigh.

And then—disaster struck.

Miss Muffins, bored with so much standing about and looking at pretty views, darted off towards another dog in the distance, catching Eleanor by surprise. The lead snapped out of her hand and Miss Muffins bounded away in the direction of the river, making Eleanor's heart go still with cold panic. With a series of joyous barks, circling skirts and walking sticks, Miss Muffins became airborne and landed with a great splash in the muddy water of the river. Only her little head was visible as she drifted away, yelping with panic and alarm. A crowd ran towards the riverbank, pointing and crying out.

'Miss Muffins!' Eleanor screamed, filled with fear that she'd lost her little friend. She ran towards the river, pushing past the onlookers. She didn't even notice when her hat fell free from its pinks and the breeze caught at her hair, tugging it free.

'Eleanor! Be careful, you'll fall,' Mary cried.

'Miss Muffins, come back!' Eleanor called. She suddenly became aware of Fred beside her. His calm stillness, his watchfulness, steadying her. He always did seem to appear just when she needed him most and there he was, like magic. She was sure he must have looked just as determined before he charged into battle. He quickly stripped away his boots and coat, leaving him standing there in his bright white shirt sleeves, making a few ladies nearby coo with admiration even in the midst of emergency. He pushed the garments into Eleanor's arms and jumped into the waters after Miss Muffins. No one seemed to notice the scars on his arms at all.

It all happened so quickly. Eleanor felt all in a daze. One moment she was chatting with Fred and Mary, the day bright around them. The sun warm overhead. Miss Muffins frisking about as usual. Then, in a snap, the dog was gone. Carried away by the water.

Until Fred was there.

The ladies around them exclaimed in almost delighted fear and cries of 'how heroic' as Mary took Eleanor's arm and whispered, 'Don't worry, Fred will get her back.'

Eleanor could hardly breathe she was so overcome with anxiety. She stood still, so very still, sure she was turning into stone as she watched Fred wade out into the deeper water and then cast off with long, even strokes to catch Miss Muffins. Just like their days of swimming in the stream at Moulton Magna, when the sunlight would glitter on his head and he would laugh and dive like an otter. He'd lost none of his skill. He reached out and grabbed Miss Muffins by the scruff of her wet neck, tugging her towards and holding her against his chest. Miss Muffins thrashed and barked, frightened that her adventure had ended so very badly, but Fred held her fast. At last, he hauled them both free of the river and stood before Eleanor, dripping great quantities of dirty water onto the grass but safe at last.

'Fred!' she cried, kneeling down beside them, her heart pounding. 'Are you all right?'

He gasped, half laughing. But he winced when he rubbed at his bad arm, as if it pained him. 'Quite so, indeed. A fine day for a swim. I'm glad I happened to be passing, Ella.'

Eleanor suddenly realised that their little drama had drawn quite an audience. She laughed, a strange little hiccoughing noise of embarrassment. 'Oh, bad Miss Muffins! Very bad indeed. Thank you, Fred. Thank you so very, very much! You have gone quite above and beyond the call of gallantry.'

'What a great hero you are!' Mary declared and a murmuring chorus of agreement flowed around them. All the ladies stared at Fred with wide-eyed amazement, as if he was the hero in a grand romantic novel.

Eleanor very much feared she was doing the same. Gaping at him—in public!—like a moonstruck schoolgirl. It was just that she was hit, yet again, with the monumental realisation that Fred was quite, quite beautiful. Even dripping with mud, his waving, bright hair plastered to his brow, he was astounding. He was so tall, so strong-shouldered, his sky eyes glowing. He was the very epitome of 'heroism' and he did not even realise it at all. Which, of course, made it all the more attractive. He stared back at her, the two of them very still, pulled together by some wild force.

Until Miss Muffins gave a great shake, sending water and mud everywhere, and their onlookers backed away, exclaiming.

'We—we should take this miscreant home,' Eleanor said. 'She needs a bath in the worst way.'

Miss Muffins howled at the dreaded *b* word. Despite her glee at jumping into the river, she hated a pan of clean, soapy water with a passion.

Eleanor ignored her, and all the new admirers of Fred still gathered around and reached out to take the dog from him.

'You'll mess your spencer, Eleanor,' Mary protested.

'Indeed you will,' Fred said. 'Let's wrap her in my coat and I'll walk with you to your lodgings. I cannot mess my attire any further, I fear.'

Eleanor glanced around. The ladies still watched in sighing admiration. Their gentlemen escorts looking quite disgruntled to lose their attention to such a heroic gentleman.

'I think perhaps we should find someplace a bit, er, quieter where I could clean up a bit,' he murmured, his face a charming, embarrassed pink at finding himself such an object of attention.

'Of course, we can go to our house,' Eleanor said and Mary nodded. They marched out of the park in a soggy little procession. Miss Muffins, far too satisfied at the havoc she had wreaked. Fred, trying to stay dignified as his footwear squeaked. And Mary barely able to conceal her delight. 'We shall have a line of ladies beating down our doors to meet Fred!' she whispered in glee, and Eleanor nodded, wishing she did not feel so very disgruntled at such a thought.

Once in their kitchen, the cook and maid set about heating water, fetching towels, scolding the pup—and clucking in concern over Fred. They took away his damp shirt, leaving him wrapped in blankets near the fire. Eleanor busied herself with warming more towels and making tea. She had to stop herself from those whirling thoughts. Wondering just what he looked like under those blankets. The strong, muscled chest that had been revealed in the wet shirt as he emerged from the river…

'Eleanor,' he said, his voice muffled in the towel. 'We should talk about what happened at the assembly…'

That was exactly what she did *not* want to do. What she had been trying not to think about at all. What she could not think about, because it was no use sobbing over what could never be. What she could not feel again.

'What of it?' she asked, busying herself with dog brushes and fresh towels, not daring to look at him.

'Ella.' He yanked the towel from his head and reached out for her hand before she could turn away from him. 'Ella, what happened…when I kissed you…'

Eleanor swallowed hard, trying not to cry. She

couldn't bear to hear his apologies, hear what a mistake it had been, even though she knew it was wrong all too well. 'I know, Fred. Truly I do,' she said quickly, looking everywhere but at him. 'There was music and starlight…it can be quite overwhelming! And memories. We are such old friends, things like that are sure to happen sometimes.'

'It's more than that. Surely you felt it, too? Felt those old bonds between us. No one knows me as you do, Ella. No one *sees* me as you do.'

Eleanor buried her face in her hands to keep him from seeing the shine of her tears at such tender words. Words she'd longed to hear from him for so long. And no one saw her as he did. No one ever had. He thought her a fairy queen, not just someone sensible and useful. He liked her as she was, just as she did him. Just as she could love him for who he was.

'Fred, I do know you and I am your friend,' she said, struggling to find the words to bring both of them back to the real world. The world where he was an earl and needed a fortune to restore his home and where she was a vicar's daughter who worked for her bread. 'And I know you need a proper wife, a lady of position. I am here to help you find her. To find just the *right* one for you and for Moulton Magna.'

'To find me a fortune to marry, you mean?' he said quietly, tautly. He tossed the towel away with a snap.

'Not only that,' Eleanor answered desperately. 'Someone for *you*. Miss Evans is a fine young lady, intelligent and thoughtful, pretty…'

Fred reached out and grabbed her hand, holding her

close. She blinked hard to keep from crying at how much she loved his touch, longed for it.

'Ella,' he said roughly. 'You are right about all that. I know it too well. But a person can't help their small dreams, can they?'

No, they could not. She was so tired from trying to force her own dreams away all the time. To stay strong. Feeling his hand on hers made her long to crumble away.

He rose to his feet and stood close to her, so very close, for that one precious moment. She dared to look up at him and saw that she had been wrong to think him beautiful earlier. He was—otherworldly. A knight from a poem in truth. How easily he overcame all her years of being sensible and careful!

Yet it could not go on. She knew it very well and surely he did, too. So she turned, cowardly, spun around and fled.

'Eleanor. Please, dear. Are you well?' Mary knocked on the door again, frantic with worry after she'd seen her sister dash past the sitting room, heard the front door close after Fred.

'I'm perfectly well, Mary, just a bit tired,' Eleanor answered, her voice muffled by distance or tears. Mary hoped it was not tears. 'I'm just going to rest this evening. Keep an eye on Miss Muffins. Make sure she didn't catch a chill after her little swim.'

'I doubt anything at all could bring Miss Muffins low. She is indomitable,' Mary said. 'Are you sure you won't go with Harry and me to the musicale tonight?'

'No, no. You and Harry go ahead. I'm going to have some cocoa and read my lending library book.'

Mary was very concerned indeed. Musicales were a wonderful time to catch up with their patrons, to make sure the right people were sitting together, and Eleanor seldom missed one. 'Shall I send up some soup later? Something warm and soothing?'

'Yes, thank you, dear. That would be most welcome.' There was a long silence, a faint rustling sound. 'Mary?'

'Yes, dearest?'

'Please don't worry. I shall be quite myself by tomorrow.'

Mary turned away and made her way down the stairs towards the sitting room, wondering what could be wrong. Eleanor was usually so steady, so practical! Could she be so concerned about Miss Muffins. But no, that could not be the whole story. Eleanor had not been herself for some days and Mary couldn't fathom it. She'd been distant, daydreamy and not as involved in the agency as usual.

Mary tried to remember what happened of late. Was there an illness in town? A match gone awry? New friends? Penelope and Fred had come back into their lives. Maybe they'd brought old memories and Eleanor just couldn't…

Of course! Fred! Mary could have slapped herself for being such a fool. Eleanor must have feelings for Fred.

And she herself had been such an insensitive looby, going on and on about Miss Evans and Fred. How ridiculous of her! She should have realised. Fred was not at all the usual agency patron and Eleanor probably had cherished tender feelings for him for a long time. What a tangle!

Mary stepped into the sitting room and poured herself a cup of now-cold tea from the pot laid out by the window where she could watch the passers-by. She took a long sip, turning things over in her mind. She was rather proud of being good at seeing how two people could fit together and make a true match. Yet she hadn't seen the perfect match right before her own eyes.

'Eleanor and Fred. Of course,' she whispered. They both had such a sense of duty, of family. They both had such kind hearts and sly senses of humour not many saw. They had a way of looking at each other when they thought the other didn't notice. Looks that were so filled with sadness and longing.

Mary sighed and sat down next to Miss Muffins, who was wrapped tightly in blankets on the settee. She listened to Harry playing the pianoforte in the next room—an echo of a sad song that reflected her own thoughts perfectly. The world was sadly upside-down now.

She'd often worried about her sister. About Eleanor's tendency to help everyone else around her before herself. She'd worried Eleanor would feel lonely and never find someone who appreciated how wonderful she was. But Mary needn't have worried at all. They just needed Fred to come into their lives again. And now Eleanor could go back to their old home, their old neighbourhood. Be the Lady of Moulton Magna…

Moulton Magna. Oh, no.

Mary's head dropped to the cushions behind her and the warm wings of hope that carried her up suddenly dropped her all over again. There was a reason Fred needed the agency and that was to find a wife who could save his home.

Miss Muffins whined as if she sensed Mary's despair. Mary wrapped her arms around the dog and held her close. 'Oh, Miss Muffins. We simply *must* find a way to assist in promoting your mama's happiness. But how?'

'What is amiss?' Harry asked from the doorway. Mary had been so wrapped in her thoughts that she hadn't heard the music cease. Harry watched her closely, her arms crossed in her elegant purple afternoon gown.

Mary shook her head. She didn't know how to begin to say everything, but she knew Harry could help. Harry's cleverness saved the agency every day. 'Oh, Harry dearest. I am ever so worried about Eleanor…'

Chapter Nine

The Theatre Royal was crowded. Every seat and box filled with flashing jewels and fluttering fans. *The School for Scandal* was still always popular and, just as at the Pump Room and assemblies, no one in Bath missed a chance to see and be seen.

Eleanor raised her opera glass to examine the throng beyond their box, taking in the swirl of pastel silks and muslins amid the scarlet velvet and gold braid of the theatre and the gleam of the chandeliers overhead. A mural of rustic Grecian muses dancing in a flower-decked circle glowed above the curtained stage. The maidens watching the furore with doubtful glares.

Eleanor, Mary and Harry very often attended the theatre, of course, as well as concerts at the assembly rooms. It was the perfect place to discreetly look in on patrons, evaluate matches, see who had recently signed the visitors' book and who might require just the right spouse. But tonight she couldn't quite focus on any of that. Couldn't stop her gaze restlessly flitting from one spot to another, one person to the next, the toe of her slipper tapping against the thick scarlet carpet. No one was the one person she most sought.

No one was Fred.

She hadn't seen him since Miss Muffins' disastrous swim, though Penelope had called to check on the pup's welfare. She'd said Fred was closeted with paperwork and agents. Eleanor longed to see him again herself, touch his hand, hear him laugh, make sure he was not exhausting himself with worry. But she knew, she told herself most sternly, it was better if they never met again at all. Not that such a thing was possible. Not if she was to find him the right match. Not if their old friendship haunted them. Yet surely, if he was truly beyond her sight, he would fade from her mind and she would one day forget him? He would be a memory, bittersweet maybe, but not a part of her life.

Eleanor lowered the glass and shook her head. Had his absence before, when he left her life and went into the Army, erased him from her thoughts? Of course it had not. She'd worried about him then. Dreamed of him. Longed for him. And she feared those things could not be ended.

Now he was even more vivid and more vital to her. More a part of her world and dreams. Even though she knew she had to help him find a wife.

'Eleanor? Look at Lady Russell's gown. Such an interesting sleeve design,' Mary said, pointing with her folded fan at the lady in question. 'Is that the latest London fashion, do you think? Maybe I should try something like that with my green striped muslin.'

'Hmm?' Eleanor murmured, blinking hard to clear

the clouds of worry, futile hope and dreams from her mind before she turned to her sister. Mary often saw far too much. 'Lady Russell's gown?'

'Those pleats on the sleeve with the gold satin insets. Perhaps it's just a cunning way to call more attention to her pearls. But I could still try it on my green. It does need some freshening up. Though I think the fashion would look better on you.'

'On me?' Eleanor couldn't help but glance down at the plain cap sleeves on her dark blue silk gown. It had been a serviceable dress for the whole season but now she wondered if it lacked any dash at all, any spark. What would Fred think if he saw her in it?

But that was beyond foolish. What did it matter *what* he thought? She had resolved to put away her feelings for him and she was going to do just that. Soon. Surely.

She *had* to.

Mary gave her a gentle smile. 'You have seemed rather preoccupied of late, Sister. A new gown always cheers *me*. Though perhaps you would prefer a new book? I am sure you've been working too hard this month.'

'No harder than you and Harry, dearest.' She pressed her fan to her lips to hold back a yawn, remembering all the late nights she'd spent recently. All the silly daydreams floating in her mind when she should be concentrating on work. 'Though I suppose I do worry about the people who are counting on us to help them find happiness.'

'As do I. It is certainly no ordinary work we do! I feel the weight of our patrons' futures, too. I want to see them all wildly happy.' She gazed pensively over the crowd, as if she matched each of them in her mind. 'Though I think there is little hope for a few of them no matter how hard we work. Can there really be a match for Mr Ormonde? And poor Lord Coulton refuses to see any lady but you. Yet we help so many! We must always remember that. See Lord and Lady Eberhart?' She gestured towards the newly married couple in their box across the way. The two of them smiling into each other's eyes as they leaned close, as if they were the only two in the whole theatre.

Eleanor couldn't help but smile to see them. Lord Eberhart had been the saddest of widowers when they introduced him to the pretty, sweet young governess and now they were as happy as two cooing doves. Yes, her work could be most satisfactory at times.

Yet there was still that tiny, sharp, wistful pang to show she would not have that with Fred. 'They *are* lovely together.'

'You knew they would suit right from the start. You always know. But you must look after *yourself* as well. Perhaps a holiday would be nice? We could take Miss Muffins to the seaside. Though I don't know if the naughty creature deserves it.'

Eleanor laughed and remembered how bedraggled and heroic Fred looked when he fished the dog from the waves. 'I am quite sure she does not deserve it! She had to have four baths to get rid of the river smell.' She wondered if Fred had needed the same. The warm, soapy water flowing down his bare back…

No. That was most definitely not a suitable image to dwell on!

'But think of how she helped us! We have had so many callers to see if she was well after her wee swim and new patrons as a result. Which is all the more reason for you to have a rest.'

'I am perfectly well, Mary. I promise. Perhaps we could go away in the autumn, once we have closed some of our files.'

And once Fred was betrothed to a suitable heiress.

Eleanor turned her head to hide her thoughts again, and caught sight of Penelope in a box down the way, her new purple and gold gown glittering. And she was not alone. Mr Anthony Oliver held out her chair for her, looking most attentive. Penelope laughed up at him, her eyes shimmering. 'Look, there is Pen! And it seems perhaps you were quite right about Mr Oliver.'

Mary gave a smug smile as she watched him sit down beside Penelope, his leg pressed to the fold of her skirt. 'They are sweet together, I think. I'm so hoping we receive an invitation to the wedding, even if they aren't agency clients. Weddings are always so lovely! Orange blossoms, cake, music, not a dry eye in the church. And when the groom looks into his bride's smiling face…' Mary sighed, a misty gleam in her own eyes as she conjured thoughts of lace and flowers.

Eleanor studied her sister in surprise. Could it be? Did Mary have match fever for herself? Her sister had always been so independent of spirit and so carefree. But did Mary actually long to wed? She did never give such an indication, even though suitors so often crowded their doorstep. Yet it did make some sense. Mary was pretty, young, vivacious and intelligent. She would make the perfect chatelaine to a fine house. A glittering hostess. If a man could be found who was worthy of her, which Eleanor doubted.

She would have to search through their files. See if there was anyone who might actually suit Mary after all.

'Oh, look, Fred is with them now! How splendid.' Mary waved happily at the box across the way, wistfulness vanished.

And so he was. Looking so handsome in his evening coat, smiling at Penelope as he took his seat beside them. Eleanor stared down at the fan in her hands feeling overly warm and flustered. How could she face him again after they let their emotions overcome them once more? How could she ever really look at him at all? Yet she had to. She could not stop herself. She peeked back to see they had all taken their seats, still watched by the ladies with their opera glasses all around the theatre.

'And who is that gorgeous giant of a man with them?' she asked once she was composed. She made herself raise her glasses to study the group again, trying not to focus only on Fred.

Mary fidgeted with her sash. 'Oh. That is a Mr Campbell, Mr Oliver's cousin. I met him at the assembly. He is a widower, guardian to a young lady who is about to make her bow in Society. He seemed rather apprehensive about the whole prospect.'

Eleanor watched him as he settled a young lady in her seat beside him and then turned to speak to Mr Oliver. The girl was very pretty, with strawberry-blonde curls and a gentle smile, but she seemed unsure of herself. 'They sound as if they could perhaps use the agency's assistance.'

'I am quite sure they could. We could surely find a wife for Mr Campbell in only a moment. Someone to help him see that Miss Adele is properly settled.' That was the sort of task Mary was so good at. Making things tidy for people. Yet Eleanor thought she saw something else in her sister's eyes as Mary studied the handsome Scotsman. Something misty and dreamy and most unlike Mary.

Penelope glimpsed them just then and frantically waved her fan at them, a bright smile curling her lips as she jumped to her feet. 'Shall we see you at the interval?' she called loudly above the roar of the theatre.

'Of course!' Mary called back.

'So much to tell you,' Penelope went on. 'Fred is quite famous!' Mr Oliver tugged her back into her seat and she turned to laugh at him merrily.

'Famous?' Mary whispered. 'What do you think...'

Eleanor studied the theatre again. There did indeed seem to be a stir rustling through the aisles and the boxes. People craning their necks and turning their glasses towards the Fleetwood box with whispers and giggles. Fred studiously ignored it all, talking to Penelope and Mr Oliver.

'He does seem to be something of an *on dit* tonight,' Eleanor said. 'What do you suppose it all means?'

'I hope it means our matchmaking task just became much easier. I didn't have time to read the papers today, so I just brought the Society pages to glance over at the interval.' Mary took a few torn bits of newsprint from her reticule and spread them on the railing. 'Hmm… The Harrison elopement. Betrothal announcements. Ah, yes, here is something!' She clapped her hands in delight. 'Look! Fred is deemed a great hero for rescuing Miss Muffins from certain watery death. Just look at this sketch.'

Eleanor was astonished. The sketch made him look like Hercules—vanquishing all opponents as he dove into raging ocean waters! She had always seen Fred's hidden gallantry, of course, even when he took pains to play the careless rogue. Now it seemed, thanks to his quick actions in rescuing Miss Muffins and the glimpse of him in a water-soaked shirt, everyone else saw it, too.

Now he would be inundated with ladies enquiring about him, pursuing him. So many thoughts passed through her mind in that moment. Delight that everyone saw what she had always known, but also sadness. Fred was wonderful and now they all saw it. She was proud of him, but also so very sad. She'd always known he could be with her, be her friend, only for a short time. Now she had to grasp whatever moments she still had. She turned away from the sight of him.

Eleanor watched the play for a few moments before secretly scanning the audience again. Perhaps that lady would do? Or that one? All pretty, all stylish, all eligible. She slowly lowered the glasses, her thoughts whirling. A decision would have to be made and soon.

She feared soon there would be one thing waiting

for them on their doorstep. A long line of ladies waiting to meet the 'Great Puppy Saviour'.

'I—I'll be right back, Mary,' Eleanor whispered quickly. She felt as if her whole being was burning with a blush, a warm yearning for something she dared not even name, and she couldn't bear for anyone to see it. To know her hidden feelings. It was as if a whirlwind picked her up and spun her about until she didn't know herself any longer.

Luckily, Mary was so enthralled by the play she merely nodded, not glancing at Eleanor, and she was able to slip out of the box into the dimly lit corridor. She hurried past a few footmen and a couple or two who lingered in the shadows. Past closed box doors until she found a quiet nook near a window looking down on the street. A carriage rumbled past. A light flashed in a building across the way. Otherwise she seemed quite alone.

She took a deep breath and opened her reticule to peek at the handkerchief inside. The folded muslin that Fred pressed into her hand so long ago and that she carried still, like a silly schoolgirl with a romantic talisman. She couldn't quite let it go. But soon, she knew, she would have to. Fred would have a wife.

She heard a footstep. A soft movement behind her and though it was so very quiet, she somehow knew it was Fred. There was a crackle when he was near. A change in the very air unlike anything else. She knew the sound of his walk, so confident and quick, the way he smelled of lemon soap and fresh linen and just that dark essence of Fred-ness. The emotions that swirled around her whenever he came close. She quickly shut the bag and pasted a smile on her face she hoped didn't look quite as false as it felt. She feared her cheeks might crack with it.

'Are you well, Ella?' he asked. His tone low and deep, filled with concern. 'I saw you leave your box so quickly.'

'Oh, quite well, thank you, Fred.' She turned to face him and saw his tall figure in the shifting shadows, the small frown on his lips. 'It was just rather warm in there and I didn't find the play as diverting as Mary.'

He nodded. 'I understand. It's been hard to be in warm, confined spaces like that since I returned,' he said simply and Eleanor wondered what nightmares lurked behind those few words. She twisted her hands tighter into the cords of her reticule to keep from reaching for him.

Yet in the end she could not help herself. She *did* reach out, gently touched his sleeve and he covered her fingers with his. He raised her hand to his lips. A kiss brushing across her fingers, hot through the thin silk of her glove. She curled her touch around him, and they stood there just like that for one frozen, dream-like moment. A moment she wished would never end.

'I—I shouldn't keep you from your party any longer,' she whispered, slipping her hand from his and stepping back even though it was the hardest thing she had ever done. 'Surely Penelope will worry?'

A smile flashed across his face, rueful and delicious. 'She is with her old friend. I doubt she will notice.'

'And your admirers?' Eleanor bit her lip, trying to

hold back that sharp prick of jealousy that touched her heart thinking of all those ladies.

He laughed. 'Admirers?'

'The ladies who think you the greatest hero after saving Miss Muffins. Which you are, of course.'

'Anyone would have done the same.'

'They would not!'

'Well, they should. A life, even one of a spoiled pup, is worth multitudes. And I am hardly a hero for it. I think Bath society merely needs something to distract it and a different 'something' will appear tomorrow.'

Eleanor thought of the agency's patrons, and laughed along with him. 'Distractions are much appreciated here, that is true. Something different from tea-drinking and rainy strolls.'

'Different from plays in stuffy boxes?'

'Different and better. For you are real.' And he was. The most real, the most beautiful, thing she'd known in so very long. Something to cling to if only she could. 'I must go.'

'Yes,' he said, sounding suddenly distracted and distant. 'We shall see you soon?'

'Of course.' She gave into temptation and touched his sleeve again, one quick brush, before she turned and forced herself to walk slowly away.

'Where were you, Fred?' Penelope asked as he slipped back into their box, thoroughly dizzy and bemused from his encounter with Eleanor. From the kiss on her hand he could still feel, like an echo deep inside of him.

'Just a quick breath of air.'

'Well! As I told you—you are the Bath *on dit* of the moment,' Penelope whispered delightedly from behind her fan as the actors gestured and declaimed from the stage. 'Isn't it so exciting?'

Exciting was not quite the word Fred would use. A blasted nuisance was more like it. When he took his usual morning walk to the Pump Room to imbibe those vile waters, he'd suddenly become aware of subtle stares and whispers. A few bolder sorts even came up to him to claim an acquaintance. Not the usual embarrassed glances he sometimes received for his scars but wide-eyed wonder from young ladies, appraising admiration from their mamas.

Some of them even spoke to him right there in the Pump Room. Soft smiles, cooing words, sweet expressions of concern for Miss Muffins. Miss Evans, or rather her formidable mother, insisted on buying him a tea, eager to hear the whole story of the 'perilous rescue'. Miss Evans was still so quiet and awkward around her mother but Fred found he liked her quiet, understanding smile and her tentative but sensible questions about his time in battle—real battle, not just dog-swimming wars. She seemed a fine sort of young lady and her mother was eager to advance their acquaintance. Yet she was not Eleanor. No one was ever really Eleanor.

He had to admit, as he glanced around the theatre, he somewhat enjoyed the admiration. In his Army years, his connection to an earldom, handsome face and thick, bright hair meant he was never short of female company. He'd never really believed their words of ardent admiration, but it was all rather fun. Then, after Waterloo, after his injuries, that admiration greatly receded. Not that he could blame them. He had healed a great deal now, but had been nothing pleasant to look at and his fortunes were quite depleted. He had to do his duty now and he'd been determined on it. He had made peace with it.

Until he found Eleanor again. The way she looked at him, seeing only *him*, Fred, none of the trailing baggage of war and injury and worry. The way she understood all without even having to speak. He was becoming addicted to her nearness. To her entrancing face, her sweet smiles and feeling the soft heat of her touch. He needed it more and more. Craved it. He feared what would happen when she was gone again from him, snapped away like some life-saving cord. Would the cold memories of war be upon him again? Could he ever escape it all?

Penelope leaned close and whispered, 'Look, there is Miss Evans in that box over there. She seems to be enjoying the play. How pretty she is when she laughs!'

Fred glanced at the young lady, who did indeed seem very interested in the antics of the actors, her gaze rapt on the stage as her mother fanned herself vigorously and examined every face in the crowd. He turned away before Mrs Evans saw him. 'She is pretty, yes.'

'And such a fine fortune her father has, they say. They also say Mr Evans is intent on a title for his daughter.' Penelope watched him carefully, as if she wanted to read something in his eyes. He so wished she would not do that.

'And what does Miss Evans say herself?' he asked.

Penelope's lips pursed. 'Not a great deal. She is a young lady who seems to keep her own counsel, which seems wise when one has such parents. They say she is often wandering about gardens here in Bath. All alone.'

'She seemed talkative enough with that young curate at the assembly,' Fred pointed out. 'And I think a little bird whispered she'd been walking with him in a garden or two.'

Penelope dismissed this with a flick of her fan. 'A youthful flirtation, perhaps. He is a handsome lad, for a curate. But, like all of us, she must listen to her family's counsel when it comes to something more important.'

'Penelope,' Anthony Oliver said, taking Penelope's attention blessedly away from Fred and his marital prospects. 'Campbell was trying to think of someplace that might amuse the young ladies, Adele as well as Grace and Natalie. We thought we might walk to the cricket green on Wednesday, if the rain holds off, watch a bit of a game, have some cake and lemonade. Charles likes to play when he can. Would you care to join us?'

'I would enjoy that very much,' Penelope answered with a brilliant smile, one Fred had never seen from her before. She glanced over her shoulder at Fred and he realised she hadn't entirely forgotten him. 'Won't you come, too, Fred dearest? You did used to admire a good game of cricket. And you were so good at it.'

He laughed, and tapped at his weaker arm. 'I used to, yes. I fear I am far out of practice.'

'This is Bath, not King's Lawn,' Penelope scoffed. 'A friendly little match, a nice outing...'

'We could certainly use any assistance we can find,' Charles Campbell said. 'We are a sorry lot, I confess, but it's all mostly an excuse for a nice walk and a cream tea after.'

'I thought I might ask Mary and Eleanor to come along,' Penelope said. '*Not* Miss Muffins, however.'

'Then I will be most happy to join such a merry crowd,' he said. And to see Eleanor again. That made him all *too* happy.

'Splendid!' Penelope leaned closer and squeezed his arm. 'I am so happy you are peeking out of your shell into the sunlight again, Fred.'

He nodded. Perhaps he was indeed. And that sunlight was called Eleanor.

Chapter Ten

Court Street Circulating Library was always most busy, but especially so on rainy afternoons. Ladies and gentlemen strolled between the towering bookcases debating the merits of various new novels, while a clutch of young poets in their corner debated a certain rhyming scheme.

Eleanor perused a copy of *The Maid of Killarney*, her mind turning over and over the theatre last night, seeing Fred there. Mary had blessedly wandered ahead in search of some ladies' fashion papers from London. Luckily seeming too distracted to question Eleanor too closely about where she had been for so long at the theatre interval. The soft patter of raindrops against the windows, the soft rustle of turning pages, the arguments from the poets, the assistants suggesting titles to two dithering matrons—it all blended into something of a song. A rhythm that circled and meandered like a river.

She sat down in a window embrasure to look over the book in her hands, pretending to be engrossed in reading.

Oh, you must snap out of this dreamy state, Eleanor! Immediately! she told herself sternly.

She had much work to do, including the difficult task of finding a wife for Fred and losing him for ever. She had to snap out of this. There was no time for any more mooning about like a schoolgirl. She was a grown woman. A woman with a business to run and she couldn't neglect it.

Thinking of the agency, Eleanor studied the room again. A shy-looking young lady stood near a collection of sermons. Maybe she needed a match to bring her out of her shell? Yet such things as other peoples' stories, usually so engrossing to her, could not distract her today.

Then she turned her head and saw Miss Evans standing by the windows with her mother.

Mary strolled over to them, her ruffled muslin skirts swaying. They were too far for Eleanor to hear their conversation, but it seemed most amiable. Mary still seemed determined that Miss Evans was the right one for Fred and it seemed she was making some headway. At least with the mother, who nodded and smiled with great enthusiasm.

Miss Evans herself fidgeted with the strings of her reticule, glancing around the library, seeming rather bored. Until she glimpsed something and her thin face lit up, making her quite pretty indeed. Eleanor wondered if it was the handsome curate from the assembly, but it appeared to be a display of botanical tracts. Most interesting. Miss Evans started in that direction, but her mother seized her arm and in a clawed grip and held her fast. Miss Evans' pretty face clouded again and she went still.

Mary returned to Eleanor, shaking her head at the tower of books at Eleanor's feet. She hadn't even realised she'd discarded so many, or what they even were. 'Eleanor! How many volumes does one need on one trip to the lending library?'

'Oh.' Eleanor glimpsed a volume of recent fashion plates and said, 'Is this not important research? We must stay *au courant* with all the new styles.'

'Indeed. Though you might stay a bit more current on millinery, sister, for I vow I have seen that bonnet you are wearing dozens of times. We must find some new ribbon at least.' Mary smoothed her gloves and nodded at Mrs Evans. 'Never mind, though. Mrs Evans seems most satisfied with the agency's progress and she would be most happy if Fred were to invite Miss Evans for a short drive or stroll.'

'Oh, Mary,' Eleanor murmured, not daring to look at her sister. 'I am not so sure Fred and Miss Evans are quite so well-matched as all that.' But she feared she was just making excuses to herself. They might like each other very well, given a chance. She could not let her feelings and old hopes sway her now.

'Pah!' Mary cried, and waved her doubt away. 'They just need to know each other a bit better.' She gently touched Eleanor's arm and smiled. Eleanor did not know what to make of the great, shining sympathy she saw in her sister's eyes, the—was it *pity*? Oh, she did hope not. She couldn't bear that. 'My dearest. I know how fond you are of Fred and you must worry about him as you do all of us. But we must do all we can for him in this matter of a suitable match.'

Eleanor nodded. Mary was right, of course. If Eleanor could not be with Fred, he did deserve someone smart, pretty and quiet-mannered, as Miss Evans seemed to be. Someone of wealth. It was the way of all things.

The door opened with a jingle of bells and Fred himself appeared there, as if summoned up by her very thoughts. With him was quite a crowd—Penelope, Mr Oliver, Grace and Natalie, Mr Campbell and his niece Adele.

'Lord Fleetwood!' Mary called, waving madly. She caught the attention of several people nearby and a wave of excited whispers wound around the stacks and shelves. Ladies patted the curls peeking from beneath feathered and ribboned bonnets, mamas urged their daughters forward, and several men looked on it all with jealous scowls.

'You see?' Mary whispered to Eleanor with great satisfaction in her voice. 'Fred's favour does grow apace! He's quite the hero now. Isn't it quite lovely?'

Lovely. Eleanor wasn't sure that was quite the word she would use. Envious, maybe, or discomfited. On her part, anyway. But it was very clear he was the latest *on dit* and how could she blame other ladies for noticing what she already saw so very well? Fred, however, looked around him with astonishment and discomfort writ large on his face. Penelope held tight to his arm and urged him forward.

Mary hurried towards their group, drawing Eleanor with her. 'What a fine chance to see you all here!' Mary said. 'Such a glorious day for reading, is it not?'

'We were planning to take the children to the cricket green later,' Mr Oliver said, with a laughing grimace at the rain. 'If the weather decides to cooperate.'

'Ah, that is Bath for you,' Penelope said with a fond glance at him from beneath her lashes, a secret little smile. But not so secret that Mary and Eleanor didn't notice, and they exchanged a significant glance. 'It always changes in only a moment. I'm sure we will be able to continue our walk in an hour or so.'

'I do hope so,' Natalie said with a pout. 'We've been stuck inside for *days* and *days*.'

Mr Campbell laughed, a hearty, deep, whisky sound that made everyone else laugh, too. Especially, Eleanor noticed with a twinge of acute interest, her own sister. Mary's cheeks turned quite apple-pink with delight. 'Hardly days, my dear,' he said. 'And surely you have been kept occupied?'

Natalie shot a disgruntled glare at Adele. 'By helping Adele practise her dancing over and over.'

'I must know the steps perfectly by the next assembly,' Adele protested. 'Or I shall quite disgrace myself at my very first public gathering in Bath!'

Eleanor carefully studied Adele. The girl seemed entirely unlikely to 'disgrace herself'. She was very pretty with her pale, silvery gilt curls and wide green eyes, her careful manners and fine clothes. She wondered if Mr Campbell sought a match for her yet, though she seemed a tad young.

'We know a very fine dancing master we can recommend, if you like, Miss Adele,' Mary said. 'Though I hardly think you must be in need of much tutelage at all!'

'My mother was a dancer who eloped with Mr Campbell's cousin,' Adele whispered, her face flaming at such a scandalous admission. 'Though I hardly remember her.'

Eleanor gave her a gentle smile. 'I am sorry to hear of your loss, Miss Stewart. But you must find a new path here in Bath! It is a fine place for it.'

'I am enjoying it very much so far,' Adele said with a little laugh. 'Especially all these books! I have never seen so many in one place.'

'And you will be much admired, I can tell,' Mary said. 'Oh, look! The sun does seem to be peeking through at last...'

Penelope and Mary had been quite right. In only an hour, the sun had crept through the pale grey clouds and shimmered over the town, turning everything honey-gold and making the gardens glitter like diamonds with left-behind raindrops. The girls' dresses, pale blue and pink and sprigged with white, looked just like the flowers as they hurried past with Adele leading Natalie and Grace and everyone else trailing behind.

It was a very merry party that set out for the cricket green, laughing and joking. Natalie and Grace skipped and pushed and giggled, admonished ineffectually by Anthony. Penelope and Mary chattered and laughed, arm in arm like old bosom bows.

Eleanor trailed behind the noisy group, the poetry

still dancing through her mind. There could be no time for poetry now. Mary was right—Fred had a job before him and so did she. The job of finding a suitable match. One that she, Eleanor, could not be.

But they did have the day, one filled with sunshine, and warmth and laughter. And she was determined to enjoy it to the full. To put it up in her memory box to take out on rainy future days.

They made their way to the cricket green at the park. The lawn undulated towards the horizon like a soft, emerald carpet, lined with flowering hedges. There was a small pavilion at one end set up with rows of chairs and tables of tea and cakes. Players ambled about, idly tossing balls, laughing and calling out challenges and Eleanor felt her spirits rise even more at the delightful scene. Once, back when she had been a youthful girl who could once in a while escape the vicarage, she'd played cricket with Fred and his brother and other young people from the estate and the village. It had been great fun, running free with the wind catching at her hair.

She sat down next to Mary on one of the folding chairs, watching as Fred, Anthony and Mr Campbell made their way onto the pitch. Fred was the first to bat.

'How can you follow what's happening?' Natalie asked, a little frown on her face as she watched the running and pitching.

'I think Eleanor knows,' Mary said, fanning herself as she studied the green. 'She used to play when we were children!'

Eleanor smiled to remember those days, running

free with Fred, the crack of the bat on a ball, the grass under her feet. How long ago they seemed now!

'Well, there are two teams of eleven players each, you see,' she said. 'With batsmen, bowlers and all-rounders. I was quite good at playing batsman and at running!'

'Like Lord Fleetwood?' Grace said.

Eleanor tilted her head to one side as she watched Fred. He had rolled his shirt sleeves up to make play easier, with no seeming thought at all to the pink scars on his skin. The strong, sinewy muscles looked as strong and as alluring as ever. There was just something about a man in shirt sleeves that made ladies' knees weak! The slight limp he sometimes showed from his war years seemed to vanish as he flew over the green and it made her smile to see him.

'Yes. The batsman and the bowler stand opposite each other on that line, the batting strip, and the bowler tosses the ball towards the batsman who then tries to hit it. If he does, he can try to run to the other end of the strip. That is called a 'run'. He scores one point for each run he can complete before the ball is returned to the field. If he's taken out, he must come off the field and can't bat again.'

'I'd like to try it!' Grace cried and Eleanor laughed as she stood up to show the girls a bit of what she re-membered using a stick Natalie found in the grass.

'There are two methods to batting, really,' she said, demonstrating. 'Vertical, like so—drive or glance. Or horizontal, sweep, square. You must watch your stance, girls, before the ball is bowled. Watch your hands, feet, head and body. Line them up like so.' Eleanor remembered all the ways to set oneself up to take a mighty swing at the ball, just as Fred once taught her. She pretended to bat then ran as fast as she could, Grace and Natalie applauding and cheering.

Her bonnet flew off but she couldn't quite care. It felt so wonderful to run once more. To feel the breeze rush past her ears. She heard cheers, and glanced over to see Fred and Anthony Oliver applauding her, Fred's face alight with laughter. She waved, laughing with them and let her feet soar. When she made the run Fred caught her hand for an instant, squeezing it.

'Well done, Ella,' he whispered. She felt a glow of pride at his words, such as she'd never known before with anyone else. 'Well done indeed.'

Mary clapped enthusiastically, barely able to keep herself from jumping up and down as she watched the wild game play out before her. It had become a beautiful day indeed. Clear, sunny and azure-sky-perfect. With the green fields rolling before them like a carpet. Laughter and cries echoed on the breeze as every care seemed forgotten and there was just a world filled with fun before them all. It was exactly her favourite sort of day—something to take such pleasure in and store up for another rainy afternoon.

Best of all was seeing Eleanor enjoying herself so much as she dashed back and forth. Her pale blue skirts flying about like those skittering clouds in the sky. Reckless and laughing and pink-cheeked. As if she hadn't a care in the world.

It was a sight Mary saw far too seldom. In fact, she couldn't quite remember the last time. Mary had few memories of their mother. It was always Eleanor who cared for Mary and her father. Indeed who cared for everyone who made their household and their agency work so very well. Eleanor who'd made sure Mary went to school and that she always had what she needed.

Mary pressed her hand to her lips, fearing she might cry just to see her dear sister look so happy. It was how matters should always be. It was what Eleanor deserved. And Mary suspected she knew the reason for Eleanor's joy now. It was plain when she thought no one watched her and she gazed at Fred with such a glow in her eyes.

Well, Mary was no child now. She knew Eleanor wouldn't see it that way, but it was Mary's turn to take charge of things of make sure Eleanor had the happy future she needed and deserved. How to achieve it, though? Eleanor and Fred were both so duty-bound. And it was true, Fred needed someone to help him with his estate. Surely there had to be a way!

'Miss St Aubin, isn't it? How fine to see you again,' she heard a man ask and she pasted on her brightest 'agency smile,' wondering if it was some patron strolling the green on such a fine day.

She turned and saw it was Mr Campbell. She was struck by him all over again. Rather stunned, in fact, to come so close to him. He was really so very, very handsome. Tall and golden and strong. Like someone in a Walter Scott novel about the noble Highlands.

'Mr Campbell,' she said. 'Indeed, yes, Miss Mary

St Aubin. How lovely it is to see you and your ward again! Are you looking for your cousin?' She gestured towards Mr Oliver on the field.

'No, not at all. He would never welcome being interrupted in the sacred act of playing cricket,' Mr Campbell said with a charmingly crooked grin. 'I was merely hoping to renew our all too brief acquaintance on such a fine, strangely sunny afternoon.'

Mary laughed. 'I see you have been in Bath long enough to know to watch for rain at every moment.'

He smiled down at her with a teasing, admiring gleam in his eye. 'Indeed. Yet, I am from Scotland and thus much used to rain. I have found that Bath has many compensations to offer for its weather.'

Mary dared give him an admiring glance in return. 'Indeed it does, Mr Campbell.'

'You have met my ward, Miss Adele Stewart?' he said and held out his hand to the pink muslin-clad young lady who'd worried about her dancing.

'Of course, we were just speaking at the Circulating Library,' Mary said with a welcoming smile to the girl. 'She was telling me how much she enjoys Bath.'

Adele flashed a shy smile. 'I—I do enjoy it very much. I like the bookshops and the milliners. And I can't wait for more assemblies. And I have joined the library, of course.'

'You enjoy reading, then? As well as dancing? What do you most enjoy? Modern poetry, perhaps, or novels?'

'Novels certainly!' Adele said with great enthusiasm. 'I love tales of Highland history, especially, since it reminds me of home. But poetry is always most welcome. Especially Scott, of course. And Mr McCloud. Have you heard of him?'

Mary nodded. McCloud was a man of meagre poetic skills but great sentiment. His work was much enjoyed by young ladies such as Adele and much aped by poets like the agency's own client Lord Coulton. Mary wondered if Adele might like him and he her in return, thus removing his romantic attentions from Eleanor. She sighed to think that probably was no solution as of yet, given Adele's youth.

'It sounds as if Mr Oliver has known Lady Fleetwood for some time,' Mary said, watching as Penelope applauded for Mr Oliver, her eyes shining.

'Yes, I believe they met when they were quite young, at some house party, but have not encountered one another again until now,' Mr Campbell answered. 'He has often spoken of her though.'

'Has he indeed?' Mary watched Penelope and then Mr Oliver with great interest. Noticing how, just as at the theatre, they seemed to have eyes only for each other. As if drawn together by some force, unable to deny it any longer. 'I do wonder why such a fine gentleman has never married.'

Mr Campbell gave her a curious glance, his head tilted as his bright hair caught the sun. Mary had forgotten he didn't know about the agency—most people did not until they required their services—and surely wondered at her interest in matches.

'Anthony is one of the best men I have ever known,' he said. 'A fine friend. A good landlord. Liked by everyone. Also an astute businessman and ruthless card player, it must be said! He deserves to be happy in his marriage. To find a lady truly worthy of their life together. It's something not as simple to find as one might expect.'

There was something in his voice, a sadness and a wistfulness, which made Mary study him even closer. He seemed distant just then, looking at the game but seeing something far away. A memory perhaps? Had he been terribly disappointed in romance? It made her feel so sad. So filled with longing to comfort him and help him.

'I am quite sure he will find such a lady. Have you ever been married yourself, Mr Campbell?' She laughed to dispel any cold touch of discomfort. 'Do forgive me! My sister says I am too inquisitive by half.'

He smiled at her. A quick, merry flash that seemed to say any dark cloud of memory had drifted quite away. 'Not at all, Miss St Aubin. You are entirely charming and a great pleasure to converse with, I must say.'

Entirely charming.

Mary felt her cheeks turn hot, a little flutter deep inside, and she glanced away to hide her burst of silly pleasure.

'And I was married once, very briefly, when I was rather young,' he continued. He glanced back at Adele, who was laughing with a group of people she had met at the tea tent. 'Not much older than Adele, in fact.'

Mary, too, studied the girl, with her smooth, peachy cheeks and innocent smile. 'Heavens! Yes, a very youthful match.'

'She was the daughter of our neighbours on my family's estate and very beautiful. I admit I was most infatuated, as any callow youth can be! But we were not truly compatible. We hadn't lived together very long. She went to London on a visit to some friends and sadly passed away soon after.'

Mary felt the sharp prick of sympathy, of sadness, for that young husband. 'I am so very sorry, Mr Campbell. Do forgive me for bringing up such a subject.'

'Not at all. It feels so very long ago now. I've been too busy with my business concerns to think of marrying again. And now I am responsible for Adele. I admit it feels rather intimidating to be a man alone trying to manage such a task as a young lady's debut!' He looked once more at Adele, who was shyly smiling up at a young man who offered her a strawberry. 'She is such a sweet, dreamy sort of girl. I should hate to see what once happened to me happen to her.'

'Perhaps, once she is a bit older and thinking of such things as marriage, my sister and I could be of some small assistance?' Mary didn't usually approach such a new acquaintance about the agency, yet something about Charles Campbell did tug at her heart. She removed a small card from her reticule and handed it to him. His hand brushed her, warm and strong through their gloves, and she held back a shiver. 'You can speak to Lady Fleetwood about us, as well. I assure you our work is much respected.'

He studied the card and glanced back at her, one brow arched. 'You are a most interesting lady indeed, Miss St Aubin.'

Mary laughed. 'Oh, I do try.'

Chapter Eleven

Eleanor glanced in the looking glass as she smoothed her hair. The brown, caramel-ish locks had been pinned up in curls and fastened with new, sparkling combs and she had to admit she rather liked the effect. It was younger, more fashionable, that she usually attempted. As was her new gown of green and gold stripes with a small frill of gold lace over the sleeves and edge of the square bodice.

A benefit musicale at the assembly rooms was always an important occasion. She'd seen many a match solidified when two people sat beside each other listening to a moving romantic aria, or walked together on the terrace at the interval. It was important to look stylish and yet respectable at such events, in case anyone needed advice or a subtle push in the right direction at the last minute.

She usually did not fuss over her appearance so very much. Tonight, though, Fred might be there and the thought that he might see her brought such a silly flutter. He'd seen her looking wild at cricket, after all!

But since he had reappeared in her life, so much had changed in her thoughts. In her heart.

It could not last, she knew that. But she had her memories back again. When he left Moulton Magna to go into the Army, she'd lost that one beautiful little thing. Now she had it back again and the memories would have to last her for a long time to come.

She smoothed her hair again and reached for her small pearl drop earrings to slide them in. She did hope he would think she looked pretty. That he might re-member, too.

There was a quick knock at her chamber door and Harry hurried in with a red cashmere shawl over her arm, Miss Muffins at her heels. The dog seemed to have suffered no ill effects at all from her swim, but would be very disappointed when she realised she would not be allowed at the musicale to make more mischief. She had quite enjoyed the attention, the little mischief-maker.

Harry, as usual, looked very beautiful in a Turkey-red and gold gown embroidered with tiny, sparkling gold sequins over the tulle skirt, small gold-headed pins flashing in her hair. Eleanor did often worry why Harry had never married again, though her friend did talk so seldom of her husband.

'Eleanor, I thought if you were wearing your red and white stripes this would look well with it but I am not sure about the green and gold…' Harry held up the shawl—a confection softer than clouds of fine cash-mere shining with embroidery.

'How kind, Harry! I think it will do quite well. I shall be quite the rare bird of colour tonight.'

Harry draped it over Eleanor's shoulders, its whisper-soft folds drifting down. 'There! How pretty you look this evening.'

Eleanor laughed. 'I did try rather more than usual, I admit.'

Harry tilted her head to the side, considering. 'Because of Lord Fleetwood? He and Penelope will be there tonight, yes?'

Eleanor glanced at her friend in surprise. Was her infatuation so very visible, then? She had to take some lessons at the Theatre Royal. 'I—I don't know.'

Harry gave her a reassuring smile and a squeeze of the hand. 'Mary and I were just looking over some of the patrons' files and she told me all about how you once knew each other at your childhood home. His name does seem to be flying around town of late! The dashing military hero who saved this little miscreant from certain drowning.' Miss Muffins looked up at her with innocent, wide brown eyes. 'We have had several enquiries about him from eligible young ladies.'

'I'm glad,' Eleanor forced herself to say smoothly, glancing down to shift some bottles on her dressing table. 'Fred deserves just the right match. Someone wonderful. Someone worthy of him.'

'As do you! My dear friend, if you care for him…'

'I cannot care for him in that way, Harry,' Eleanor interrupted. She could not bear to hear such things any longer. She had this one evening. She didn't want to mar it, no matter how well-meaning she knew Harry and her sister were. 'You know why he came to the agency. The condition of his estate.'

Harry nodded, her eyes too understanding, too knowing. 'There is always more than one solution to a difficulty, I have found.' She picked up Eleanor's small strand of pearls and helped her fasten the clasp. 'Mary was also telling me about Penelope's old friend, Mr Anthony Oliver. She believes they are also very fond of one another. Very fond indeed.'

Eleanor nodded, relieved at the change of topic and the focus on someone else's romantic life. 'I do think they are. I have never seen Penelope look so happy. She had quite the burden with old Lord Fleetwood.'

'I made a few discreet enquiries about Mr Oliver.'

'Harry! You know he is not a patron.'

'Perhaps not, but Lady Fleetwood is a friend of yours, yes? Mary said we should help her if we possibly could and I agreed. We must make some use of our contacts once in a while.'

'Yes,' Eleanor admitted. 'I agree we should help Pen if we can.'

'Well, Mr Oliver has made quite the fortune. He is a man of property, quite daring in his investments. He owns a fine house in London and two country manors he has made very profitable. He is also highly respected by all his business acquaintances and employees and is considered very eligible. He is also, as we can see for ourselves, most handsome! If he and Penelope come together...'

'What do you mean?'

'I mean, surely he would wish to help his new wife's

family if he could. His fortune is quite great, all built up himself.'

Eleanor considered this and it was as if one tiny, shimmering ray of hope light broke through. 'Harry. I hadn't thought, that is…'

'It was just a thought, of course. An idea that we might help more than one patron at a time, which is always a pleasure.' Harry picked up Eleanor's small bottle of lavender water and gave her a spritz. 'Mary was also telling me she met a man called Charles Campbell, kinsman to Mr Oliver, and she wonders if he, too, might like to find a suitable wife. And one day a match for his ward.'

Eleanor considered his, her professional instincts taking over. 'Yes, Mr Campbell does seem a fine gentleman. Handsome with a Scots accent I'm sure many ladies would appreciate! And his ward, Miss Adele, is very mannerly and pretty but at a rather impressionable age. I would think he must be rather struggling with it all. A single man with a girl to bring out in Society. He seemed most amiable.' She remembered something else—how Mary looked as she laughed with Mr Campbell at the cricket green and her bright pink cheeks. 'Mary did seem to like him.'

Harry looked most thoughtful as Eleanor watched her in the looking glass. 'Did she now?'

The music room was already crowded when Eleanor, Mary and Harry arrived, sans the distracting company of Miss Muffins. The pale yellow walls shimmered in the light of dozens of candelabras from the glow of the crystal chandeliers overhead and the air smelled of lilies and roses from the silver-potted arrangements banked around the low dais where the musicians warmed up. The gilt chairs snaked in lines around the display. The most well-known people of Bath sat the front, the ladies' gowns shining like stained glass and their jewels gleaming.

'Eleanor! Over here, do come sit with us,' Penelope called. She sat on one of the back rows with Mr Oliver. The two of them leaning very close—or possibly that was Eleanor's imagining, brought on by Harry's romantic speculations about the pair. Yet they did seem comfortable and happy in one another's company. As if they had always been just so. 'Fred had another appointment this afternoon but he promised faithfully to be here before the music begins, so I have saved him a seat. Eleanor, do sit between us here. You can find him when he arrives. Wasn't the cricket delightful? I vow I miss a bit of fresh air at times! We must have a picnic at Beechen Cliff again soon.'

Beechen Cliff—where Fred had caught her when she fell, and she had never felt more safe, more cherished. But she was saved from having to answer, to have her blushes noted, when the conductor appeared on the stage. The musicians lifted their bows amid applause and launched into their first piece—a Handel air. The notes were flying through the air like summer swallows when someone sat down beside Eleanor. She knew right away it was Fred. No one else felt as he did, smelled of that lemony sunshine. She trembled knowing this was it. This was the one last time she would truly let herself feel for him. Be with him. One last memory.

'Do forgive me,' he whispered to Eleanor, his smile rueful and bright as the sun to her. 'Pen will surely be angry I was so late.'

'They have only just begun. She said you had a business appointment?'

'Yes, with the family's attorneys. The estate agent is to arrive tomorrow.' Fred grimaced. 'I am sure he will tell us dire news and give me instructions to retrench most severely.'

Retrench—or marry well? Just as she, and everyone else, knew he must do. Yet the reality of it was so cold. Like a sudden, drenching rain. 'Do excuse me,' she gasped and dashed out of her chair and from the crowded music room. She hoped Mary or Harry would not follow, for she had absolutely no words to explain herself.

She made her way past a few couples strolling the corridors outside the concert room, nodding and smiling as if all was perfectly ordinary and her heart was quite whole and content. Or at least she *hoped* it looked that way. She'd had such long practice in hiding her emotions, making a smooth and smiling facade, surely it must work now.

She turned and moved onwards, half blindly, down a staircase, past a row of pale classical statues that watched her with blank, indifferent eyes. It made her feel invisible. Like she could crawl away and no one would notice except these gods and goddesses who did not care one whit. She wasn't quite sure where she was going, perhaps looking for a withdrawing room, but really she just wanted that moment alone. A moment where she didn't have to hide her feelings for Fred.

She turned once more, and found a half-open doorway to a dark room beyond. It seemed to be a storeroom of sorts, with crates stacked along the walls. Perfect. She tiptoed inside and leaned against one of the boxes, taking a deep breath as minutes ticked past.

Suddenly, she heard soft footsteps in the corridor outside, pausing as if they too looked for a hidey-hole. She held her breath, listening to them come ever nearer. A shadow loomed in the doorway, elongated against the flagstone floor. A hand reached out...

Eleanor gave a soft, involuntary shriek. But then she blinked and saw it was no stranger or ghost that had found her. It was Fred. Fred—the one person she longed for, the one she was trying to escape. He was shadowed by the luminous lamplight behind him, yet she knew it was him. No one else felt like that or smelled of summer sunshine like him.

'Blast it all, Fred, you frightened me,' she gasped.

He flashed her a rueful smile, white in the shadows.

'I'm sorry, Eleanor. I was worried when you left the concert so suddenly.'

'I—I needed a breath of air.'

'I agree. It was quite crowded in there. So much—noise.'

Eleanor remembered what he'd told her of his time in battle. The noise, the chaos, the feelings of despair. Perhaps he did sometimes feel overwhelmed now, and didn't speak of it. Couldn't escape it. She reached out and gently touched his arm, hoping he saw that she understood.

He covered her hand with his own and she felt the warm steadiness of him envelop her until she couldn't even remember her own fears.

His eyes narrowed and his expression turned serious, intent, as he studied her. He slowly, carefully, reached for her other hand and drew her closer, as if giving her the chance to draw away, apart from him. She could not. She seemed bound in a silvery net of enchantment. Fred wouldn't ever look like her everyday world, grey and practical, her feelings hidden. The feelings she had with him were as bright and wondrous as a vivid summer day.

She swayed closer to him, and wound her arms tightly around his neck so he couldn't fly away again and leave her alone in that dream. She wished she could stay in his embrace all night—every night! To forget about duty and families. Everything but him.

She stared up at him in the shadows, thinking how beautiful he was. Even his scars made him more so, with what they said about his honour, his heart.

'How lovely you are, Fred,' she whispered.

He gave a surprised laugh. 'Of course I'm not. I am quite a wreck.'

She shook her head. How could she ever convince him of what she saw, what she'd always seen, in him? She went up on tiptoe and pressed her lips to his in a swift, sweet kiss, as if it could say what she could not.

He groaned and pulled her closer, so close there was not even a breath between them. He deepened the kiss, his tongue gently seeking the taste of hers and she fell completely into him. Lost in that wild need to be just that close to him. Drawn to him by those invisible, silvery magic cords that had always seemed to bind them together.

She didn't question herself. Couldn't walk away. Not yet.

He pressed tiny, soft, fleeting kisses to her cheek, her temple, the tiny, ever so sensitive spot just behind her ear. She shivered to feel the warm rush of his breath on her skin.

'Oh, Ella,' he whispered hoarsely. 'How can we go on like this?'

She nodded, leaning her burning face into his shoulder. She tried to breathe deeply, but that only seemed to draw him into her even more, surrounding her with his very essence. He was the one true thing she'd always clung to. She saw that now. Yet soon he would have to go away from her, for always.

She imagined nights in the future, when she would lie alone in bed, listening to the silence beyond her window. When she would close her eyes and remember Fred just as he was now. Remember how this felt. She leaned her forehead against his chest and listened to the steady sound of his heartbeat. She let it flow through her and bind them together. She hoped it would be enough to hold them together at least in some way for a long time to come.

She kissed his cheek one more time, and spun

around to leave. 'Thank you,' she whispered and dashed away. At least she would always remember how his kiss felt. Always.

Chapter Twelve

'And this portion, you see, Lord Fleetwood, is quite a large parcel and is not part of the entail set up by your great-grandfather,' Mr Palmer, the estate agent who had travelled from Moulton Magna with parcels of documents and surveys for Fred to study, said as he pointed out a detailed map of the estate.

It was vital work. Under his father's lackadaisical final years of stewardship, the property had become very disorganised indeed. Farms required vital repairs, fields and structures were neglected. Finding any assets that could be sold was most important, it could tide them over until Eleanor's agency found him a suitable heiress bride.

Eleanor.

The sweetest, kindest, most beautiful lady he could hope to know. And one as far from him as the moon, despite the heated rush of her kisses and the way she felt under his touch. That kiss had been nothing else he'd ever known. It had sent him out of himself, out of the world entirely, and shown him a heavenly beauty and sweetness. A perfection. He'd thought of little else since…

'Lord Fleetwood?' Mr Palmer said, breaking into his longing, lustful thoughts.

'Yes, of course,' Fred said quickly. He studied the map before him and saw not what was now, the neglect and decay, but what had once been and what might have been. Fine farms, fertile fields, a home for so many. But all that would take funds.

He examined the outlined parcel to the north of the estate. It was indeed quite large, with properties to make up a fine manor of its own for a buyer or tenant. It would still leave Moulton Magna with its oldest portion, its grand house and the home farm that could be made productive again. Yet he remembered that land so well from when he was young. The stream, the fields and woodland. Running there free with Eleanor, the happiest he'd ever been.

'What was meant for this land here?' he asked, tapping his finger at the largest parcel of the north manor. He remembered when he was just a small boy and his father managed to purchase it from the neighbours as the last puzzle piece to the estate. His father had ridden there with small Fred in front of him in the saddle, pointing out the prettiest spots to him. There had been an old manor house, in need of repair but pretty, and empty meadows. 'I'm sure it was not meant to be left vacant when it was acquired.'

'Indeed, no, Lord Fleetwood. I believe your mother planned to make the old house into a school for the children of tenants and employees,' Mr Palmer said.

He took off his spectacles, gave them a polish before replacing them on his nose and harrumphing. 'A very kind lady she was. I remember your father's widow, the current Dowager Lady Fleetwood, was once minded to revive these ideas. It would be of great benefit to so many, but by then there were not the funds.'

'Of course,' Fred murmured. So many things left undone. So many regrets. 'But the land could be sold?'

'Certainly. The terms of the entail only include this central portion, the house and home farm, and these tenant farms here and here. These acres were acquired later, of course, as was this woodland. It would be a shame to lose them. I believe much could be made of them with the proper planning. But these unfortunate circumstances do happen.'

Fred nodded. Unfortunate indeed. They were all trapped by the past now. By choices others had made.

He suddenly longed to know what Eleanor would think. What she would advise.

The door opened, interrupting his thoughts and dreams. 'Why, Mr Palmer!' Penelope said as she hurried into the library, holding out her hand for the delighted estate agent to bow over. She was dressed to go out, in a dark blue redingote and feathered tilted hat *à la militaire*. 'What a lovely surprise to see you today.'

'And a pleasure to see you again, Lady Fleetwood,' Mr Palmer said with another little bow. Penelope had been so popular at the estate, even in the midst of his father's worst behaviour. 'I brought some of the newest surveys for his lordship to review.'

'Yes, of course,' Penelope said with a sigh. 'Always

the worry of Moulton Magna.' She leaned over to study the map. 'Is this portion where the school was once to have been built?'

'Indeed, my lady.'

'Such a great pity. It would have been of such value.' She looked most wistful for a moment, quite far away, before she gave her gloves a sharp tug and put on a bright smile. 'I am going to meet Mary St Aubin at Molland's. I shall be back for dinner tonight. Then to the theatre?'

Fred had forgotten about the theatre. He had been so much in crowds of late, so many people wanting to meet him now that he was the 'heroic celebrity' of the day for rescuing that silly dog and he longed for a quiet evening by the fire. But he knew he couldn't do that. A wife had to be found and contacts made if they were to dig themselves out of this mess. He rubbed wearily at his eyes. 'Yes, of course. And we can talk about that masquerade you're so excited about, as well.'

'Oh, my dear Fred. You've been working so hard,' Penelope said, gently touching his hand in sympathy. 'You must be so tired! But I promise the masquerade will be fun. Just what you need. Some music and light, wine and pretty ladies.'

'Maybe you're right, Pen.' Once, when he'd been young and careless, he'd thought *fun* would solve everything, too. It hadn't, of course. It had only created new problems. But maybe the music and noise would stop him thinking so very much right now. Stop him thinking too much of Eleanor.

Penelope took a parcel from under her arm and

handed it to him. 'Here's a black cloak and mask for you, as I know you won't wear a costume. Now, I really must fly. So charming to see you again, Mr Palmer.'

Once she was gone, Fred made himself study the maps and ledgers that so limited his future again. 'Now, Mr Palmer, do show me these figures again…'

Molland's was quite busy when Penelope pushed open the door, with every table and stool occupied. But Mary had saved seats near the window where they could watch everyone hurrying past.

'Penelope!' she called with a wave. 'Over here! I have marzipan.'

Penelope threaded her way across the room to sit down across from Mary at the high table, gratefully accepting a cup of tea. It was not at all a long walk to the shop, but every step had felt weighted with thoughts and worries. Seeing Mr Palmer and all his maps and papers just brought it back to her what a mess they were all in. How unfair it all was on dear Fred.

Mary smiled, and gazed out of the window as she waited for Penelope to collect herself, calm and unhurried. Penelope was happy to have such friends in the St Aubin sisters. She'd not often had female friends, except for Miss Collinwood who had once taken her to that house party where she met Anthony Oliver. Friends were the best part of her new life in Bath. A life she could create for herself for the very first time.

Now, though, she feared she and Mary together had got something very wrong.

'I'm sorry I was late,' Penelope said, popping a bit of

that divine marzipan into her mouth. 'Mr Palmer, an estate agent from Moulton Magna, was there with Fred.'

Mary gave her a sympathetic frown and offered
more tea. 'Is the news so very bad, then?'

'No more than I had imagined. But, oh, Mary! I do
fear so for poor Fred. For his future happiness.'

'Don't worry, Pen, darling, I beg you. I have a fine
idea for him, a very pretty young lady whose parents
came to the agency on her behalf, a Miss Evans. Her
father is a businessman, quite well-to-do, who is eager
to find a titled gentleman. She would help him to put
all things to right in no time. If they like each other.'

Penelope sighed. 'I'm afraid that is quite the trouble.
I know of the agency's fine work, of course, that is why
I sought out your help…'

'But?' Mary gazed at her curiously, not at all angry
or worried.

'But I quite fear Fred is in love with someone else.'

Mary's eyes widened. 'Is he indeed? But that is
lovely! Someone suitable, I hope? It is not a regular
occurrence, I admit, but we *have* had people come to us
in despair they should never meet their match and then
they find them all on their own. They merely needed
reassurance, I think. It's a good thing!'

'That is the very problem.'

'She is *not* suitable?' Mary gasped. 'An actress or…'

'No! No, the lady herself is most suitable. She merely
has no fortune and Fred feels he is bound to take on
the whole burden of his family and estate.' Penelope
took a deep breath and tried to find just the right way

to state her concerns. 'Mary—did you ever have any suspicions about Fred and Eleanor?'

'*Eleanor?*' Mary burst into laughter. 'Fred and Eleanor? No, I surely would not have…' Suddenly, her laughter broke off and her eyes grew even larger. 'Oh. Of course. Yes. I did wonder but then I thought…what a great fool I have been. How quiet she has been lately and how they look at each other. Oh!'

'Then you see it, too?'

Mary took a long, flustered sip of tea. 'I did not before. I was too intent on agency business. So sure my instincts would lead me to the right answer.' She pounded her gloved palm on the edge of the table. 'How silly! How could my instincts have failed me with my own sister?'

Penelope sighed. 'Perhaps our instincts are sharpest when we are not so very close to the situation.'

'I truly should have seen. At Beechen Cliff, the assembly, the cricket.' Mary shook her head. 'Poor, dear Eleanor. She has been so distracted of late. So distant and—and sad. I feared she had been working too hard.'

'Fred, too, has been distracted and solemn. Most unlike his old self.'

'Well, then, he cannot marry Miss Evans, or anyone but Eleanor! Love is truly the most important thing, if one is lucky enough to have it. I would never see my sister made unhappy.'

'Nor can I bear to see Fred sad. He was a true friend to me when we first met and when I needed one. But his sense of duty would never allow him to abandon his estate.'

Mary scowled. 'What a dreadful conundrum. Yet there must be an answer, if I look hard enough.'

'I have thought of one.' Penelope drew in another deep, steadying breath. She'd realised what she had to do on her walk to Molland's. And the sparkling, hopeful way she'd felt when Anthony Oliver didn't, *couldn't*, matter one bit. 'You must find me a match. The most wealthy gentleman you know. It does not matter his age or—or anything else. As soon as you can.'

Mary looked horrified. 'No, Pen! You must not rush into such a thing. You deserve happiness, too. I'll find you someone. Indeed I will. But not like this.'

'It *must* be like this. I can't let Fred and Eleanor give up their love if I can help them. I heard Mr Palmer say Fred could sell a parcel of Moulton Magna and use the money to repair the main house and revitalise the home farm. If I had a husband of fortune, surely I could include buying this land in our marriage contract and then I could be of help often after. Fred just needs some assistance to start his work. And Eleanor would make him the finest of wives.'

'Of course she would. Eleanor would make any man worthy of her love the most fortunate man living! Yet surely Fred would never see you make such a sacrifice.'

'Then we must do it without telling him. He'll only find out once the match is made, so we must work quickly.'

Mary still looked doubtful. She glanced wistfully into her teacup, as if she wished it could be something a tad stronger. 'I will go and look at our ledgers right away, and put off Miss Evans somehow. I can find you someone, Pen, I am sure. But working so fast…'

Penelope held up her palm. 'A fortune. That is all he must have.' She thought of her past husbands, old men who gambled and drank and who saw her as a prize to be displayed. And of Mr Oliver's kind smile. She had to forget that now.

Mary sighed, and nodded sadly.

'Now,' Penelope said with determined cheerfulness. 'Let us talk about the masquerade at Sydney Gardens! One last glorious burst of merriness for us all. I intend to dance my slippers off and consume an immoderate amount of rum punch. Tell me, Mary, do you have your costume yet?'

Half an hour later, Penelope departed from Molland's amid a light, grey drizzle, sad but most determined. She parted with Mary on the corner of a busy lane, and watched as her friend hurried back towards the agency to study their ledgers of patrons.

A flash of colour caught her attention and she paused to study a bonnet in a milliner's window. Bright blue, with purple and pale blue feathers and fluttering lavender taffeta ribbons, like an exotic bird suddenly alighted on a plain stone wall.

She imagined herself wearing it. That colour following her on her path to bring noise and commotion and *life* again. It had been so long since she'd had such things amid days of worry, helplessness and loneliness.

In fact, she couldn't quite remember when she last had such colour in her life at all. It had been a very long time indeed.

She tugged at the edge of her old grey hat, and smiled to imagine it turned to blue instead. That she was a young lady who wore the latest styles, who could laugh and dance and flirt without a care. She suddenly did remember when she last had such a life, if only briefly. It was that house party where she danced in the moonlight, played croquet and lounged in the sunshine.

With those memories breaking around her as if they were yesterday, Penelope turned and strolled on, thinking not of Lord Fleetwood and all those solitary days at Moulton Magna as his wife and widow, but of the present day and the present moment. Maybe she wanted everyone she cared about to be free and happy because once she had seen such things for herself. Felt the wonder of falling in love, the giddiness of spending her moments just as she liked. She couldn't have held onto them then, yet surely Fred could. Dear Fred, who gave so much in the Army, who cared so much about his home. He deserved happiness.

She came around the corner of her own street—and found herself face to face with Anthony Oliver. The Anthony of her memories and the man she longed for still. He smiled and swept his hat off to reveal windruffled, glossy dark hair and she couldn't quite breathe.

His smile widened and for an instant she was flying right back to those days of youth and laughter.

'Lady Fleetwood,' he said with a bow. 'What a fine chance to see you today.'

'And you! But please—call me Penelope when we meet like this? It would make me feel rather like myself again. Not this stuffy old matron I seem to have become.'

'I'm honoured, Penelope. If you will call me Anthony, as you once did.' He paused, his smile turning wistful, as if he too thought of their sunny days at that party. How they seemed so close and yet so far away. 'And I dare say you are the least, er, stuffy lady I have ever known. I remember at that house party, when you insisted we slide down the stairs on silver trays as if we were sledding!'

Penelope hid her laugh behind her gloved hand. 'Oh, I do remember much about that dear party! It has always been a memory of such a happy time.'

'For me, as well. The happiest.' For a long moment, they merely watched each other. Silently. Intently. Watching time trace itself backwards between them.

He offered her his arm. 'Shall we walk for a while? I am still learning my way around Bath.'

'As am I. I should much enjoy a turn with you, Mr Ol—Anthony.' She gazed up into his eyes, like warm, amber sherry. He must have had many ladies in love with him since they last met. 'If I am not detaining you from an appointment.'

'Not at all. I promised Natalie and Grace I would take them for ices, but not until later. I am quite—free.'

Penelope smiled, wondering if that could be true. If they were both at last free. 'As am I.' She slid her hand over his sleeve, feeling his muscles tense under her touch, and she longed to lean into him. 'Your nieces are so charming.'

'Indeed they are. I fear they quite have me wrapped

around their fingers. They like to dress my hair in curling papers, use me to boost them up trees they are not meant to climb and make me a fourth at dolls' tea parties.' He sighed theatrically. 'I am much put upon.'

Penelope laughed, picturing him at a tiny table with a wee tea set, his hair curled. What a fine father he would make! It gave her a pang to realise he had no children of his own yet. 'You like children?'

'Very much. Especially clever ones like Natalie and Grace.'

'So do I. As often as I could at Moulton Magna, I visited our tenants' children, played with them and read with them, I loved it. They made me laugh like no one else could!' She sighed to think of the school she had longed to build for them, which could not come to pass.

He studied her from beneath the brim of his hat, those sherry eyes sympathetic and warm. 'You have none of your own?'

What would have sounded like the veriest impertinence from someone she'd just met merely seemed like empathy and understanding from Anthony.

'I should have liked to, but it was not meant to be.'

And, despite her disappointment, it was fortunate she had none with her dreadful husbands. She was not tied to them in any way but memory and that faded when she was with Anthony. 'But you, Anthony! I am sure you would make a most fine parent indeed. I wonder you have not married.'

He gave a wry laugh, looking away. She glimpsed a spot of red blush on his cheekbones—most intriguing and sweet.

'You and my sister! I am forever fending off her "helpful suggestions" and "chance meetings" over tea tables.'

Penelope thought of the agency and thought it was good his sister had not yet seemed to have heard of them. Anthony would be snatched up in a moment if he sought their services! 'You have met no lady to suit you?'

Their steps slowed, ceased, and he looked down at her without blinking. Without turning away. 'Indeed I have. That has long been my trouble.'

Penelope could not breathe. Her heart felt so tight, so hopeful, so panicked and wondering. 'Did—did you?'

'Yes. Long ago, I saw a young lady, with dark eyes and a sweet smile, who made me laugh as I never had before or since. Made me *feel*, as I certainly have not done since! I could not forget her. No one else has ever equalled her.'

'I—understand,' she whispered. 'When I was young, I also found a person I was most drawn to. Most—intrigued with, truly. I thought then it was only a dream. A vision that would fade in the face of reality…'

He stepped even closer, taking her hand in his. 'As did I. I worked as hard as the devil for years. Threw myself into my business. Built it to where it is, trying so much to forget.'

'And did you ever? Forget?'

His fingers curled tighter around hers and she hoped most fervently he would not let her go. Not let her fall. 'Never. And when I saw her again, at Beechen Cliff, I knew I never could have forgotten at all. She was all I remembered. All I longed for and more.'

Penelope gave a tiny, choked sob, letting herself believe again at long last. Letting herself hope. 'I never forgot, either. When I was unhappy, in despair, I remembered those days with you. The laughter and dances. The feeling that I could say anything at all and you would understand.' She rested her forehead against his shoulder, listening to the steady, reassuring beat of his heart, uncaring who might see them. 'I thought I would never see you again.'

And here they were, together, nothing between them now. She felt giddy, dizzy, so young again! She felt like herself.

He laughed, and raised her hand to his lips for a long, lingering kiss. The warmth of it flowed into her cold, lonely heart and made it summer again.

How could she ever deny such feelings to anyone she cared about? To Fred and Eleanor? She had to help them. Had to make sure the world was put right for them all.

Chapter Thirteen

'Oh, Eleanor, isn't it terribly exciting?' Mary whispered as they stepped through the gates of the gardens into the fairyland of the masquerade everyone had been looking forward to all the social season.

'It is,' Eleanor agreed, surprised at herself. She could seldom afford to be fanciful, to whirl around in girlish excitement, but she felt the fizz of it all inside herself tonight. The gardens, where they so often walked, had been transformed into something astonishing. A dream world. Equally dreamy creatures drifted past them—fairies, elves, queens and kings and knights. Mysterious men in black cloaks, faces hidden.

Here, she did not have to be Eleanor. She could be anyone at all. She could escape work and worry for a time. Though she found she could not escape thoughts of Fred. The memory of their kisses, the way he made her feel, the way he made her forget all she'd worked for, strived for and tried to be. With him, she was not sensible. She was—free.

Mary held her arm tightly as they followed the butterfly-bright crowd down the entrance pathway towards the main theatre set up near the centre of the gardens—their destination for the evening. Through the carefully spaced trees, thousands of coloured glass lamps faceted to make the lights sparkle like stars and cast amber, green, blue, red over the costumed crowds flitting between them.

Eleanor smoothed her own skirt, dark red and black velvet made to look like a Renaissance duchess's, and straightened her red satin mask.

'Oh, look at that man over there!' Mary whispered with a giggle. She tugged at the edge of her white, pleated muslin Greek goddess costume, looking like an angel of white and gold. Eleanor felt such a burst of pride in her beautiful sister. 'See? The one dressed as a medieval knight. Such delicious broad shoulders! Can we entice him to the agency if he is unmarried? He would be much sought-after.'

Eleanor laughed, but she was quite sure the knight's shoulders were not nearly so fine as Fred's. She remembered how those shoulders felt under her touch when he caught her at Beechen Cliff. And how strong he was when he saved Miss Muffins from the river, and made himself an idol to every lady in Bath.

Eleanor suddenly stumbled a bit on a loose patch of gravel on the pathway. Cursing her silly, distracted state, and her new heeled shoes, she yanked her heel free and hurried after Mary.

A stage surrounded on three sides by temporary wooden boxes was the centrepiece of the party. Four classical colonnades held the supper boxes, wrapped by more shadowed walkways and trees. An orchestra played on the stage, lilting dance music to greet the guests who cried out to friends and looked around for new flirtations, trying to guess who was behind the masks.

Even more of those glittering lanterns were draped everywhere, lighting up the colonnades so brightly it could have been midday. The magical costumed creatures floated through it all, catching Eleanor up in the dazzling kaleidoscope.

She was so distracted, she stumbled again and someone caught her arm before she could fall. Dazzled by it all, she glanced up to find it was one of those black-cloaked men. A plain satin mask covered most of his face, his head draped in a hood, giving him a slightly sinister air in the midst of that fairyland.

Instinctively, she drew back a little, startled. But then she glimpsed the eyes behind the mask, bright blue and realised how very familiar that touch felt through her velvet sleeve. Surely only one man felt like that. Smelled like that, made her heart race like that.

'Thank you, F—that is, sir,' she whispered. He nodded and let her go, disappearing into the crowd before she could stop him. She wondered if she had only imagined him there.

'Hurry up, Eleanor, we'll fall behind!' Mary called.

Eleanor shook away the strange, fantasy spell of the gardens, of the man who might or might not be Fred and followed her sister to their designated box. It was a small space, open on one side so they could watch the dancing in the centre, made even closer by the long table and close press of chairs. Penelope and Mr Oliver waited for them, dressed as Eleanor of Aquitaine and a knightly swain, along with Charles Campbell, dashing in his kilt and Adele in a pretty, ruffled pink shepherdess gown and beribboned bonnet. A few other friends had joined them and to judge from the clutter of empty wine bottles on the table and their loud laughter they'd already begun the revels. They called out merry greetings and offered glasses.

'Here, Eleanor, do try some of this punch,' Penelope urged. 'It's quite fine and they've brought us such a great quantity.'

Unlike the food, Eleanor thought wryly as she studied the scant, small platters of cheese and ham, with a bit of shrivelled-looking fruit. They clearly hadn't gone to Molland's for the catering.

She took a sip of the offered punch, which was an inviting bright pink colour in the Venetian glass vessels—and coughed as her eyes started to water. 'Yes, it's…er…quite good indeed.'

And it rather was, once she'd got past that first sharp kick. Rather sweet, really and most relaxing. She sipped some more as she studied the passing crowds. She wondered if each man in a black cloak—and there were many—could be Fred. Surely she should have followed him! But then what would she have done if she found him? She was meant to try and forget him, not chase him over the park! But if he spoke to her, touched her…

Eleanor sighed. She knew she could do none of the things she dreamed about.

The orchestra launched into an aria and the famous soprano Signora Boldini appeared amid enthusiastic applause and cries. She held out her arms and curtsied deeply, vast white plumes nodding in her upswept hair. She threw back her head and launched into her song. A tale of love lost, won and lost again. Of heartbreak and longing. A tale that soon had everyone sighing just to hear it, just to feel those words in their own hearts.

Eleanor's eyes suddenly prickled with tears that threatened to fall at any second. She stared down into her empty glass, blinking furiously in hope that no one would see her silly weeping. It felt as if the walls of the box were closing in on her. The press of other people was so much she couldn't breathe.

'I'll be back directly, Mary,' she whispered.

Mary glanced up from whispering with Mr Campbell, her eyes wide. 'Are you quite well, Eleanor, dear? You look rather flushed.'

'I'm perfectly well, just—just need the necessary,' she blurted, unable to think of a more dignified excuse. She slipped out of the box, away from the music and the well-lit walks. She glimpsed couples flashing in and out between the trees, so close to each other.

She felt dizzy and rather silly and so very sad. Could it be the melancholy song? The punch? She really didn't know where she was going. She only knew she had to be alone for a moment, to collect herself.

She saw a narrower, darker path just ahead and stumbled towards it on her new shoes. There were far fewer lamps there, just a sprinkling set high in the trees, and it was blessedly quiet. She heard whispers and soft laughter beyond the trees, yet could see no one else. A cool breeze brushed over her warm cheeks.

Up ahead, in a clearing, she saw the white marble of a little teahouse where Mary and Miss Muffins liked to stop sometimes for a respite on walks. It was much like the one she remembered at Moulton Magna, where she and Fred could meet secretly and be comfortable and happy for a little time. She turned towards it, sure it would give her a peaceful place to sit for a moment and her heel caught again in the gravel. This time, it caught her off-guard completely and snapped off to send her tumbling towards the gravel pathway.

There was no time at all to panic or scream. A strong arm caught her around the waist and lifted her up and up, the trees spinning over her head. Cold fear rushed through her like ice in her veins, freezing her in place. She'd heard the tales about such parties before, surely she should have known better than to wander off on the dark paths by herself! Now surely something dreadful was going to happen.

She kicked out wildly, but her feet caught in her heavy skirt and pressed her even closer to her captor. She twisted and tried to scream and by sheer luck her fist flew backward and connected with a solid jaw.

'Ella! By Jove, I think you broke my tooth,' a man growled in a low, rough voice. A familiar voice.

'Fred!' she gasped, appalled she had just planted *Fred* a facer. 'What on earth…?'

'I saw you walk away from your box and you looked upset I suppose. I wanted to be sure you were all right.' He slowly lowered her to feet, holding her steady until he was sure she could stand on her own. She wobbled a bit on the broken heel of her shoe and inhaled deeply, smelling the warm, comforting scent of his lemon soap. How could she have mistaken him for anyone else?

He rubbed at his jaw. His face was all sharply carved lines and angles in the shadows. His hair was tousled. 'Oh, Fred, I am sorry I hit you.'

He laughed ruefully. 'You do have a strong right hook, Ella, no doubt. And good for you using it! I should certainly have called out to you. I had no business surprising you like that.'

'Still...' She gently reached up and touched his cheek, feeling the prickles of his afternoon beard on her palm and the heat of his skin. 'It may be quite black and blue tomorrow.'

'I shall just tell people I rescued another pup from certain doom. It will surely enhance my heroic reputation.'

Eleanor studied him for a moment. The shadows were deep there amid the trees, but a stray strand of silver moonlight fell over him, gilding him, erasing all the years and trials that had stood between them, making him her young, darling friend Fred again. He had discarded his mask and his eyes glowed like a summer sky. She remembered her feelings when she arrived at the masquerade. That she could be or do anything for this one night. What if she was not Eleanor, the vicar's daughter, the matchmaker and he was not Frederick the Earl?

'Well, thank you for catching me again,' she said. 'How clumsy you must think me! It was just too warm in the supper box. I needed a bit of fresh air.'

'Most understandable,' he said. 'The crowds are overwhelming tonight.'

'Yes, exactly. And I'm afraid I let Penelope urge too much punch on me. I was quite giddy.'

He laughed, the most delightful sound, and it made her want to laugh, too. Made her want to spin around and dance! Everything did seem grander tonight. Larger. Brighter. 'Too much of the punch, eh? I fear I know the feeling well.'

She sighed to think of the two, or maybe it was even *three*, glasses she had consumed.

'What was in it?'

'Quite simple, I think, a few grains of elderflower mixed with sweet wine and rum.'

'Simple yet deadly. Is that how you came to stumble?'

'I am not as ale-shot as all that, Frederick!' she said indignantly. 'I stumbled because my new shoe broke. I knew I shouldn't let Mary persuade me to wear them, but she said I could certainly not wear my old dancing slippers with this costume. What a difficult time Renaissance ladies must have had!'

'Let me see. Let's sit down over there and I'll see if I can fix it. At least well enough to get you home without a turned ankle.' He gestured towards the little teahouse, which was softly lit by a few lanterns that flickered over its pale walls, making it look like a piece of the moon.

Eleanor nodded and leaned on his arm as he led her towards its open doorway. The one round room inside was empty, but furnished with a few cushioned chairs and settees, lit by those lanterns and the open rotunda over their heads. He helped her to sit down, and knelt before her like a gallant knight with his lady. He gazed up at her with steady expectation as her heart thundered inside her, his blue eyes glowing.

'Are—are you a cobbler, too, then? As well as an earl and a soldier?' she whispered.

He gave her a wide, flashing smile. The smile that always did such strange, twisty things to her stomach. 'I am a man of many talents, Ella.'

'That I do know.' She felt that odd, bemused spell he cast come over her again and she didn't feel quite in control of herself. She slowly lifted her hem a few inches, and held out her foot.

Fred slid a strong hand around her ankle, his fingers strong and warm through her stocking. She shivered as his caressing touch slid over her instep, tickling lightly as if he touched her bare skin. It was so shocking, so...

Delightful. Better than all her dreams of him had ever been.

He slid the velvet shoe off her foot and examined the cracked heel of it as he still cradled her foot in his other hand. She had never imagined she could feel that way from someone touching her mere foot. Feet were merely utilitarian, of course. Meant to carry a person about and not be very attractive. But Fred touched it as if *her* foot was something precious.

She felt so dizzy all over again, and reached down to balance her palms on his shoulders. Yes—they were finer than the man Mary admired earlier, for certain.

The feel of those hardened muscles shifting beneath her touch did nothing to steady her at all.

'I am afraid it is quite hopeless,' he said.

'Hopeless?' she gasped. Yes, indeed, *they* were hopeless and always had been. She could not feel this way about him.

And yet, at this moment, she had never felt more right.

'Your shoe is beyond repair,' he said.

She laughed. 'You truly are not a cobbler, I see.'

'I am a man of some talents, but master of none.'

'I find that hard to believe,' she murmured. He was truly a master in the art of touching a woman in a way that made her mind go all soft and dreamy. Every soft little caress he ran over her toes and the arch of her foot, made her shiver. 'How am I to walk on the broken heel?'

'Well, one of the talents I learned in the Army is improvisation.' He slid the shoe back onto her foot and gently placed it on the ground. Then he reached for her other foot, curling his fingers around her ankle. He removed her other shoe. 'Hold on to me.'

That she could gladly do. She curled her fingers tighter over his shoulders and he let go of her. He twisted hard on the intact shoe heel and broke off that heel, as well.

'There! Slippers. Very fashionable,' he declared.

Eleanor laughed. How very silly she felt suddenly! 'Then you are a master cobbler indeed.'

'I try my best to right any wrong that comes my way.' And Eleanor knew he truly did. He was an honourable man, no matter how he protested, and would never let anyone who relied on him be disappointed. She loved that about him, even as it kept them apart.

He reached again for her foot and Eleanor giggled, some imp of mischief that usually hid deep inside of her peering out. She tucked her foot further in the folds of her skirt, making him search through satin, velvet and lacy muslin petticoats to find it.

When he caught her ankle he drew her closer to him and her fists curled on his shoulders. She closed her eyes against the sensations his touch created in her, his hands sliding along the curve of her leg. She felt him press a shocking, heated kiss to her ankle and she gasped as her eyes flew open. She felt weak and hot and collapsed onto the floor beside him, sending them both off-balance and tumbling down.

Fred caught her before she could hit the stone floor and lowered her slowly, slowly, bracing his hands to either side of her head. He gazed down at her, silently and intently, and all she could see were those wondrous eyes.

No one had ever looked at her as he did. As if he saw all of her, right down to her heart. She reached up in wonder and touched his cheek, traced her fingertips over his lips. At last, he lowered his head and pressed those lips to hers. It was so soft and slow, almost gentle, as he brushed his mouth back and forth over hers pressing little kisses to her lower lip. Those slow caresses ignited something deep inside of her, some burning need only Fred ever brought out. She curled her hands into the folds of his cloak and dragged him closer, opening her lips under his.

He groaned deep in his throat and the kiss changed. Became more frantic, more filled with need. She could taste him. Wine, and mint and the night air. Her palms flattened and slid around his back to hold him with her as long as she could.

His lips traced from hers along her cheek, below the line of her mask, to the line of her jaw and then to the soft spot behind her ear that made her gasp. It was like ripe summer fruit bursting over her tongue and she sought his lips again, so eager for another kiss.

Barely had their mouths touched when something broke through her dreamy haze—an explosion high over her head. It took her an instant to realise it was a *real* explosion, not one in her heart. Her eyes flew open to see fireworks through the rotunda above them, red and blue and bright white in the night sky. The party was winding to its conclusion and the flames seemed to illuminate what she was doing. The mistake she was making.

She pushed him away. His blue, blue eyes, incandescent by that firework light, went wide with a shock that echoed her own.

'Ella,' he said roughly. 'I'm so sorry…'

Eleanor frantically shook her head as she pushed herself up from the floor. She never wanted to hear his apologies, his regrets. She was never drinking punch again that was for certain.

'I should find Mary and the others,' she managed to say. 'They will be missing me.'

Fred stood up and held out his hand to help her to her feet. She let him, but released him as soon as she could.

'Let me see you back to the supper boxes.'

'No, no!' Eleanor cried, gathering her gown closer around her, smoothing her skirts and her hair. 'I—I am fine, I promise.'

'I know why you wouldn't want to be seen with me,' he said. 'But let me follow at a distance and make sure you get there safely.'

Eleanor almost laughed. Dear Fred, always gallant and kind. But her most *unsafe* place was surely right here with him.

'You will not even know I'm there,' he said.

She knew he would do it anyway. 'Yes. Very well.' She spun around and left the little teahouse, turning back towards the colonnades. 'You're going in the wrong direction,' he offered.

'Of course I am.' She spun back around to study him one more time. Her tousled, golden knight. 'Oh, Fred. You should marry Miss Evans, you know.'

He frowned fiercely. 'Miss Evans?'

'The pretty heiress. You need her and…' And Eleanor needed Fred. Always. The one thing she could not have.

She turned on her broken shoe again and headed in the right direction towards the lights and music. Towards reality again. She dared to peek back to see if Fred followed her, but he was nowhere in sight. She seemed to be alone once more.

Chapter Fourteen

'Don't you think, Lord Fleetwood?'

Fred glanced down at Miss Evans as she walked beside him, distracted from his ever-distant thoughts. Sydney Gardens had been cleared of signs of the masquerade. The boxes torn down. The dance floor taken away. The lanterns had vanished. Yet he could not forget that night at all.

When Penelope and Mary suggested they might meet Miss Evans, the lady Eleanor urged him to marry, and begin to see if she might be a suitable countess, Fred gave in against his every instinct. They were right, everyone was right, that he had a duty. And Eleanor had her own responsibilities, even if she *was* the only lady he had ever longed for this way.

Yet Eleanor surely would not have him. Her sense of responsibility too strong. *His* sense of responsibility too strong. Miss Evans was a quiet, pretty and well-mannered lady of fortune. Eleanor's urgings made real-world sense, of course.

'I do beg your pardon, Miss Evans, I fear I was wool-gathering,' he said. He glanced up ahead at where Mrs

Evans walked, her purple-striped parasol bobbing, too far to hear them.

Miss Evans nodded solemnly. 'Business matters, no doubt.'

He laughed at her knowing tone. 'A bit, yes.'

'My father is the same. I am sure it must all be so worrisome.' She studied the paths around them in the weak, watery sunlight, twisting the handle of her parasol. 'I do often wish Father would teach me more about it all. His business that is.'

'Do you indeed?' he said, surprised. In his experience, young ladies rarely wanted to know about balance sheets and outgoings.

'It might liven things up. Things are so dull otherwise.'

Fred gestured to the crowds around them, the horses and carriages on the promenade beyond, the display of fashion and conversation. 'Is life in Bath so very dull, then?'

Miss Evans gave him another of her inscrutable, serious glances. 'Not dull for someone like you, perhaps, Lord Fleetwood.'

'Someone like me?'

'Someone who has seen so much of the world. They say you were in the Army. I envy you that.'

'You envy Army life? I fear it is nearly always a lot of dull, uncomfortable waiting with a few moments of acute terror in between.' To say the least. 'And very little good food. The salt beef and biscuits on march are appalling.'

She laughed, surely something she did not do often.

Her dark eyes sparkled and Fred could see why Eleanor might urge her on him. But he could only see her with a certain indifferent admiration, a sort of curiosity. She seemed different than what he might have expected.

'Not really the Army, I think, but just to *see* things. Other cities and lands, different people. Making choices for yourself.'

Fred nodded. Yet look what such *choices* had brought him and his family. To the edge of ruin, to the point of having no choices at all. 'It is not at all the glorious adventure books and poetry might say.'

'Of course not. But at least you have *had* choices. And you have the memories of those sights and sounds and experiences. I have never been able to choose anything at all. Not even this bonnet I am wearing.'

Fred, puzzled by her intense, almost despairing tone, studied the chapeau in question. 'It is—very pretty.'

Miss Evans nodded gloomily. 'But it is not *my* bonnet. All these feathers and bows! It's my mother's. I do hate the bows.'

Fred thought this over. Was he like the bonnet, then? Someone else's choice that she would have to live with? What did she want instead? Travels? Another gentleman? What did *he* want?

He knew what he wanted. Yet he could not have that. He assuredly empathised with Miss Evans. 'What would you choose to do then, Miss Evans?'

Her solemn expression changed like the sun from beneath a cloud, her eyes shimmering, a smile touching her lips. And her answer surprised him.

'I would *choose* flowers! I would travel the world

and find rare botanical specimens and record them in my sketchbooks. I once had a governess, you see, a wonderful lady called Miss Montgomery, who saw how much I loved our botany studies. She had a brother who worked at Kew Gardens and he came to give me a few lessons, too. He gave me books to read and the names of botanists I might correspond with who would answer my questions. It was all so wonderful! I was never happier. Then my parents found out.' Those clouds slid over her again.

'I am sorry,' Fred said.

Miss Evans peered up at him with a little frown. 'Are you?'

'I am. To have something that means so much to you taken away in an instant...'

Miss Evans sighed. 'I must admit, Lord Fleetwood, you are much more amiable than I would have suspected.'

Fred felt a warm little touch of amusement at her evident surprise. 'Am I really, Miss Evans? I am not called "amiable" very often.'

'Oh, but I am sure you are. I thought you would be like my parents. Consumed with your own needs and ambitions and unable to see anything else. Yet you seem very understanding.' Her steps paused on the walkway and she studied the ladies far ahead of them, the tall plumes on her mother's hat waving emphatically as she insisted on something to Penelope and Mary. 'Lord Fleetwood, may I be honest with you?'

'I wish you would.' He thought of all the artifice in life, the veil that covered too much. He wanted to shout his feelings for Eleanor to the world, to send everything else to perdition, but he knew he could not. He could not even speak of it to anyone.

'I know well that my parents wish us to marry. It's why they came to Bath, after all. I suppose they imagined it might be easier to secure a title here than in London.'

Fred stared down at her. She was honest indeed. He couldn't help but like her. 'I am not sure, Miss Evans, really. I think…'

She waved his words away impatiently. 'It does not matter, Lord Fleetwood, for I know them well enough to see their intentions. Yet I think you might have feelings for someone else.'

Fred felt all topsy-turvy suddenly, as if he had been tossed into the air and landed in a new, strange, honest world. 'I…' He feared he was stammering like a fool again, but he wasn't sure what to say.

'I vow I do understand, Lord Fleetwood. We all have so many obligations to our duties, to people we care about and they often conflict with our own hearts. And I do love my parents, even if they can be quite ridiculous about matters like these.'

'We do have duties, yes, Miss Evans.' Yet somehow those worries felt a little lighter, just to be able to say those few words to someone who seemed to see them for what they were.

'Then I say we try this, Lord Fleetwood. I know you have many admirers after heroically saving that little dog from drowning, I hear your name everywhere I go. As does my mother.' She waved at her mother, who was peeking back at them curiously. 'You can marry in a moment, yet I sense there are other things you might wish to pursue and I would not care at all. You could have my dowry, which really is quite large, and my father would have your title. I could study and you could return to your estate and be with your true love, whoever that might be. It could all work out so very well!'

Fred had to admire such a plan. Matter of fact, shrewd, rather brilliant actually. It would be a good plan indeed, if he loved a woman who could agree to be his long-term, quiet mistress. But it would not work with a respectable vicar's daughter like his Eleanor.

'Miss Evans,' he said. 'You are a wonder, truly. And I admit it is a very fine idea.'

Her eyes narrowed. 'But?'

'But I fear the lady I do love could not live like that. She is too respectable. And I couldn't ask you to live like that, either. For all that we have just met, I admire your spirit and independence. You deserve your studies and travels just as you wish.'

She shook her head, but her eyes were kind as she studied him. 'It is a good plan, I know. But it is also a bargain and I would want to offer you the chance to make free choices, too. If your love is a fine lady...'

'She is. Very.' And she was the only one he would want. The only one he had *ever* truly wanted, Fred saw that so clearly now, like a lightning bolt. He could never find even a shred of happiness if Eleanor was not near. He had to be with her. He had to find a way. Think beyond the strictures, as Miss Evans did. 'Just as you are.'

'Then we must be friends. I need as many of those as

I can find.' She went up on tiptoe and kissed his cheek. They heard a faint gasp and titter from her mother but Miss Evans just smiled coolly. 'Are we, then, Lord Fleetwood? Friends?'

'I would be honoured, Miss Evans.'

She took his arm and they strolled onward, amid all the watching, gossiping stares of the garden pathways. 'Do you perchance know of any other titled gentlemen in such a situation, then?' she asked, most practical. 'Someone kind, of course, who would not object to a studious wife. I have made the acquaintance of a very handsome young curate who might suit my purpose, but alas it would not be so easy for my father to accept him…'

Eleanor could barely believe what she was seeing. It was as if the sunny day had suddenly been covered by grey clouds, a wind sweeping coldly over her.

Miss Evans kissed Fred on the cheek, in the middle of the Gardens, and now they linked arms and strolled onward, laughing together most comfortably. Like old friends. Or a new couple.

She felt the sharp prickle of threatening tears at her eyes and she angrily dashed at them with her gloved hand as Miss Muffins peered up at her in concern, whining low in her throat.

'I am quite well, my dear,' she assured the pup, but Miss Muffins tilted her hear doubtfully. Eleanor even doubted those words herself, though she knew they had to be true. She had to be well. To move forward. She had told Fred he should marry Miss Evans. She couldn't be unhappy that he had taken her advice.

And wasn't matching Fred with an intelligent, attractive young lady like Miss Evans what she wanted? They could be a good couple, each having what the other needed. And a good-looking couple, too, producing fine new earls for the future.

She turned away and walked as quickly as she dared in the opposite direction. She could not give Fred what he needed for his estate, his title or his duty. She had only her own energy. Her mind and thoughts and imagination. She had her love for him, too. That love had always been there. Would always be there. Miss Evans had a fortune and she was an interesting lady. Eleanor liked her, too.

Yet those moments at the masquerade…

'Fool,' Eleanor berated herself as she walked. She'd always known this day would come, ever since Penelope asked for the agency's help in finding Fred a proper match. She'd especially known it since Fred rescued Miss Muffins and became quite famous. Every eligible lady in Bath admired him now!

Yet knowing it and facing it as reality seemed two different things. She'd dared to let herself dream for a moment. Surely she knew better than to do that? Hadn't she learned in her life that dreams were not for ladies like herself?

Any time she had with Fred, time to see him or talk to him, grew shorter and shorter now. She had to steel her heart to give that up. To go on with her life as before. She'd been content with that. With work and her sister and friends. She could surely be content again? Even though she knew, deep down as the truest thing ever, that she loved him and would always carry that love as her great secret.

And that love was exactly why she had to give him up. He needed so much more in life than she could give him. It was simply reality. And no moonlit masquerade would erase that.

She nodded and smiled at friends and agency patrons as she passed them near the gates. Trying hard to pretend, to them and to herself, that all was well. That her heart was not cracking to bits inside of her.

Chapter Fifteen

The next day Eleanor forced herself to rise, even though she'd barely slept a wink, and dressed quickly to make her way downstairs for a quick breakfast and then work. Work would surely distract her from thoughts of Fred. It *must* she determined and made her way out of the room, with Miss Muffins at her heels, turning towards the staircase in the still-quiet house.

She almost missed the step as she saw him in the foyer below, looking so radiantly handsome standing there in a ray of sunlight from the high windows. She clutched hard at the banister.

Somehow she'd thought, in the imaginings of her sleepless night after seeing him with Miss Evans, that she would encounter him again in a crowd. There would be no chance there of a private word and she could prepare herself. Put on her armour of dignity and duty.

Now there was no chance to prepare herself at all. He was *there*. He glanced up and saw her, staring at him with unguarded, starry-eyed, raw love.

She snapped her gaping mouth shut and tried to smile politely. She feared she failed terribly. So many

emotions flooded through her. All the things she had
denied, pressed down, for so many years. All the longing of her soul to reach out to his.

'Eleanor,' he said eagerly, hurrying to the foot of the
stairs with a smile on his lips. 'I know it's very early to
call, but I've been waiting for you. I have to talk to you.'

To tell her he was marrying Miss Evans? Eleanor
swallowed hard past her distress at the thought. 'Have
you?' she managed to say. She forced her feet to keep
walking down the stairs.

'I have to say—so many things.'

'I know we must talk, yes,' she answered softly.
It had been foolish to think she could ever dismiss
her feelings for him in a crowd. This was *Fred* who
had been her friend and her love for so very long. She
couldn't hide from him.

'Shall we?' He gestured towards the door of the
small sitting room just off the agency office.

The early-morning silence of the house seemed so
large around them and Eleanor feared she couldn't trust
herself to be alone with him there. To be close to him,
alone with him. Yet she couldn't run. She nodded, and
hurried into the room.

It was seldom used except when she, Mary and
Harry needed a consultation over patrons. It was very
feminine and frilly—all pale green and pink, small and
close and friendly—and she knew it was a mistake to
be there with Fred. He was too close, too warm and so
strange and familiar all at the same time. The scent of
his lemon soap flowed all around her.

She plopped down on a pink-cushioned settee and

folded her hands tightly in her lap, trying to look anywhere but at him.

'Eleanor, I…' he began, then broke off with a rueful laugh. He ran his fingers through his hair, leaving it standing on end, shimmering in the sunlight from the window. Eleanor had to clutch her hands even tighter to keep from giving in to her longings and reaching up to smooth it and feel the silk of his curls against her skin.

'I fear I am no good at this,' he said.

'You came here to say that you are marrying Miss Evans,' she blurted.

His eyes widened and for a moment he just stared at her in taut silence. 'What? I—no…'

'It is quite all right,' she rushed on, wishing so much this was all over. 'You need not say anything at all. I know how things must be. We do part as good friends, I promise.'

'Part?' He shook his head fiercely, and sat down beside her to reach for her hand. She dared to let him. Dared to feel his touch just once more. 'Eleanor. No. That is not what I want at all.'

Eleanor feared she would burst into tears. She tried to draw away from him, but he wouldn't let her go and she couldn't give him up. Not yet. 'Then what is it? You have found someone besides Miss Evans?'

He looked amused. *Amused*. 'I rather hope so. Oh, Eleanor. I told you I am terrible at such things, but surely we have known each other so long, so well, that we *know*. I—oh, blast it all. Eleanor St Aubin, will you do me the great honour of being my wife? I fear I have no ring yet, but I shall do. This very day.'

Eleanor was shocked, cold and hot all at once. She had never been so entirely at a loss in all her life. Surely she had not heard him correctly? 'Fred? Marry you? What?'

He frowned at her doubtfully. 'I know I have little to offer you, but we can start again once I sell off the land at Moulton Magna. We can retrench. Rebuild. And once I return to the Army there would be that income.'

'The Army?' Eleanor gasped through her daze of joy and despair. What was happening? Yet she could hear that—he intended to return to the Army. After what had happened to his friend? The terrible things he had seen? 'You cannot do that. Moulton Magna needs you. You belong there now.'

'But that is why I will return to my commission. To earn what I can. If you are at the estate all the time, I know I can do that.'

'And that is why I cannot let you do that! Even if...' Even if he wanted to marry her, which had always been her deepest secret dream. Her greatest hope. She loved him too much. 'Your duty is to restore your home and we both know I have no fortune to help you. I have nothing to offer you, as Miss Evans does.'

He shook his head again. 'Eleanor. You know that is not true. You're the kindest, sweetest lady I have ever seen. You love Moulton Magna, too. I need you by my side! After what happened at the masquerade, I know we both feel this between us.'

The masquerade. The finest, most wondrous night of her life. But that had to be behind her, a mere dream. She wanted to hold on to what they had as long as she possibly could. That invisible, silvery line between friendship and love had snapped, but which she longed to repair. To have something she could clutch at.

As she looked into his eyes, those sky-blue summer eyes she had loved for so long, she caught a glimpse of what life could be like with him by her side. Yet there was such danger in wanting something so very much it hurt.

'I will not use that to tie you down to something you will come to regret,' she said. She tried so very hard, with all her might, not to think about all the long years that stretched between that moment with him beside her and life without him. 'We can have no future together, can we? I will not let you return to the Army. You must find a wife who can be all you deserve. Which I am certainly not. You would come to resent me one day. I know it.'

His eyes shone like glass, as if he might start to cry as she longed to do. If he cried she knew she would be utterly lost.

'But I cannot live my life without you. You are my other half. You have understood me as no one else ever has or ever could. When I am with you, the world is always bright. Always just as it should be! With you—I know I can achieve anything. You do not have to tell me how I feel for you, Eleanor. I know very well. I have always known.'

'Fred,' she choked out, knowing she would be lost if she looked at him again. And they would both be lost if she gave in to what she wanted for so very much. 'You would hate me!'

'You know I could not. You are *Eleanor*. My friend. My love. My true love.'

'Fred. No.' She could say no more.

'Please,' he whispered. He reached again for her hand, but she buried it in her skirt. 'I *need* you.'

Unable to bear being near him a moment longer without throwing herself into his arms, taking what she wanted and not what was best for him, she leaped to her feet and turned her back so she couldn't see his face. 'I told you, Fred. I care about you too much to ever let you down in any way. To keep you from what you must do.'

She shook her head hard to be rid of what she longed to say—that she loved him. She loved him with a force and fire she'd never believed possible. Every time she saw him that love grew stronger. That was why she had to let him go.

She leaped to her feet and threw open the sitting room door to run out. Hurrying up the staircase, she dared to glance back, just once. Fred stood in the doorway, watching her with that tousled hair and desperate eyes. Could he, did he, love her as she did him? She had never expected that, hadn't expected that he would *want* her to stay with him and it broke her heart all over again.

She spun around and ran onward, past a gaping Mary and Harry and a startled Miss Muffins, and didn't stop until her chamber door was locked behind her and she could fall down in tears.

'Whatever are you doing, Mary?' Harry whispered.

'Shh!' Mary whispered back to her friend, not even

glancing over her shoulder from where she knelt beside Eleanor's closed door. She pressed her ear closer to the wooden planks and waved Harry closer.

She sat down on the carpet beside Mary in a puddle of pink muslin skirts. 'What is amiss with Eleanor?'

'I'm not sure, but I can guess. I just saw Fred leave with a face like a thundercloud and now poor Eleanor crying her eyes out.' Mary listened carefully to Eleanor's muffled sobs and she was sure her own heart would crack to hear her dear sister so destroyed. 'I fear it is all my fault.'

'Your fault, Mary?' Harry whispered. 'How so? You and Eleanor adore each other. You always do what's best for one another.'

'Yes—and so I should always have put *her* needs first!' She told Harry all about how she had urged Miss Evans and Fred together and that now Penelope was determined to marry a wealthy old man herself to make sure Fred was free. 'I should have seen it all along! I never should have tried to force things as *I* thought they should be. I have been doing this work too long.'

'Oh, Mary, no.' Harry wrapped a comforting arm around Mary and they sat huddled there together, longing to make all things right as they occasionally passed fresh handkerchiefs under the door to Eleanor. 'We run a *matchmaking* agency and our task is to assist the people who come to us for help. To give them what they say they need. We cannot read their minds! If Lord Fleetwood changed his desires…'

Mary nodded, still miserable. She knew Harry was quite correct. They were in the business of settling advantageous matches for those who couldn't do it for themselves. Yet she had always prided herself on her rare instincts and her intuition for romance. This time she had been a fool.

'Fred and Eleanor belong together! They've always been meant for one another. But I know my sister. She will never be selfish if she thinks it's for the best for him.'

Harry gave a little huff. 'Well, Eleanor *should* be a bit selfish for once! She's always been the kindest of friends, the most soft-hearted matchmaker of us all, but she's taken on too much responsibility for everyone else in her life. *She* deserves something now!'

'Exactly,' Mary sniffed. 'How can we make her see that? How do we get Fred back for her now?'

There was a brief knock at the front door and Mary sat up straight in a burst of hope. Perhaps Fred had *already* come back!

It was not Fred, though, who came hurrying up the steps but Penelope. Penelope—another kind soul who had tried to sacrifice herself for the people she cared about. To throw away her happiness for others. And Mary was sure now she had ruined everything for *all* of them!

'Whatever is happening?' Penelope cried, taking in the closed door and the bedraggled figures on the floor. She drew off her gloves and plopped down on the carpet beside them.

Mary disconsolately told her all they knew about Eleanor and Fred and Miss Evans, until they all collapsed in tears again.

'Oh, my dears,' Penelope said, leaning against them until they feel into a heap of muslin and wool and feathers. 'I do think that this once *I* can be of some help to *you*!'

Chapter Sixteen

'Fred, dearest! Do come in for a moment,' he heard Penelope call as he tried to slip out of the house without being seen.

He knew he had been an utter bear for days, ever since he parted with Eleanor, yet he couldn't seem to stop himself. He was in no fit state for polite society. Unable to think of what to say. Forgetting all he had relearned after his recovery from battle wounds about polite behaviour. Instead, he went walking alone all hours of the day. Up and down hilly streets, through parks and up into the hills. Prowling aimlessly. Trying to outlast his thoughts. But they wouldn't be left behind. Wouldn't stop replaying memories of Eleanor at every moment.

He did love Eleanor for so many reasons, one of them being her kind heart. For as long as he'd known her, she'd put so many people before herself. Her father, her sister—and now Fred. She thought she did what was best for him. He knew very well that was her reasoning. But how could any of it be right when it felt like *this*? It was worse than being wounded and lying on a battlefield. Worse than the cold rain of endless, lonely marches. Worse than the pain of sword strokes and canon shots. Eleanor was the brightest light in his life. In all the world. Finding her again had made him feel hope once more. Hope that there might be some happiness out there. Some contentment and fulfilment in life. A purpose. A family.

Eleanor knew and accepted him, as he did her. Surely that was rare—to be seen, cherished and accepted. Everything else could be solved as long as he had her and had her help. If only he could make her see that together they could bear anything!

Instead, he prowled the town alone, like that wounded bear and Eleanor seemed to have vanished.

He saw how Penelope watched him, with such concern in her large eyes. Yet he didn't know how to reassure her. Didn't have the words to make it all clear to her—or to himself. So he started avoiding her, too.

Now she stood in the drawing room doorway, catching him before he could vanish out in the grey day.

He glanced back at her, attempting a smile. He could see that she was not fooled. She tilted her head, studying him with that concerned little frown he'd come to dread.

'I was just, er, going out on an—important errand. Most important,' he said.

'Yes, so I see. This will only take a mere moment Fred and it is quite important.' She turned in a swirl of blue silk skirts and disappeared back into the drawing room.

Fred slowly followed. He knew he had been brusque

with Pen lately and he hated that. She'd always been a true friend to him, an ally in his family, and she deserved his confidences about all that had happened. If he could only find the right words. Perhaps he would be forced to do that right now.

Yet when he stepped into the sunny chamber, he saw Penelope was not alone. Mr Palmer, the Moulton Magna estate agent, sat behind a writing desk surrounded by papers and ledgers. Alexander Oliver was also there, standing near the windows. He turned, a pleasant smile on his face, his eyes glowing as he saw Pen and she rushed to him to take his arm. Fred felt a burst of hope that maybe this wasn't about his misery after all, but about some secret happiness of Penelope's.

'I am so glad you could join us at last, Fred,' she said. 'Anthony and I have several bits of news to share and Mr Palmer has kindly agreed to stay in Bath and help us with our business before he returns to Moulton Magna.'

'Mr Palmer?' Fred said, still puzzled.

Mr Palmer nodded before scribbling on.

'Indeed.' Penelope glanced up at Anthony, a radiant smile on her lips. 'I am sure you can guess, but Mr Oliver has asked me to marry him and I have agreed.'

'At last!' Anthony said with a merry laugh. 'I've waited for this glorious moment for *years*.'

Penelope laughed, too. They couldn't stop staring at each other, as if they'd forgotten anyone else was there at all. It gave Fred joy, as well as prickling jealousy, to see them.

'He is so patient,' Pen said. 'I, too, have waited. Though I was sure such a day would never come.'

'Pen, there are no words to tell you how very happy I am for you,' Fred said, leaning over to kiss her pink cheek, once so pale and thin. 'No one deserves this more than you.'

Penelope grabbed his hand. 'Except for you, Fred! You deserve all joy and happiness, too. You deserve to know this feeling—the promise of a happy family life.'

Fred shook his head. That feeling, that hope, had sunk away when Eleanor turned away from him. 'I am sure I will, one day, if I am very lucky.'

'No, *now*.' Penelope glanced up at her fiancé. 'Fred, darling, I know you shall think we are terribly interfering, but I know you do love Eleanor St Aubin. And that she loves you.'

Fred stiffened. 'Pen...'

'Fred, just listen. You and Eleanor should have every happiness. You have both given of yourselves for others much too long.' She gave a rueful grimace. 'I think we *all* have been trying to sacrifice ourselves to help each other lately! I'm so fortunate now that I can actually do something to help.'

'Pen, whatever you are about to do, I'm sure I can't let you,' Fred warned.

Anthony laughed. 'I don't think you can possibly stop her, man! I have learned very well that once Pen has an idea, she will not be stopped.' He gave her a teasing, smiling look that said he would never *want* to stop her.

'And this is hardly a sacrifice anyway. It is merely sharing my joy,' Penelope said.

Fred studied her suspiciously. 'I think you had best explain it to me, then.'

'Of course.' Pen waved towards the chairs grouped around the desk. 'Mr Palmer is here to help us.'

Mr Palmer glanced over the edge of his spectacles, looking almost cheerful for once. 'You are a most fortunate man, Lord Fleetwood,' he said, carefully arranging the papers around them.

'Am I?' Fred said, utterly bemused. He hadn't felt 'fortunate' in a very long time. Perhaps never.

'Oh, indeed. Lady Fleetwood and Mr Oliver have brought their marriage settlement for us to examine and there is one provision that should greatly interest you.'

Fred studied Penelope, who looked much too rosy and self-satisfied. 'Interest me?' He felt quite like a parrot now, repeating every sentence.

'Yes. It seems Lady Fleetwood and Mr Oliver wish to purchase the east parcel land at Moulton Magna to create their own estate. For a most generous sum. Quite high enough to set Moulton Magna on the firm path to self-sufficiency again. With the essential work from your side, of course. The estate requires much modernising.'

Even more confused, Fred turned to Penelope, who beamed back at him. 'We shall be neighbours, Fred! At least for part of the year.

Anthony laughed. 'If you can stand us!'

'Why would you want to be at Moulton Magna?' Fred asked her. 'Surely you were not happy there.'

Penelope shook her head. 'It is true I was not very happy in my marriage, but I cared very much about the people on the estate. Like you, they were so welcoming and kind to me. I always felt terrible I didn't have the resources to build that school as I wished. But now I can! With your permission, of course.'

'You wish to buy the land and improve on it?' Fred said, his thoughts racing over new plans as he studied the map and envisaged a new future.

'To build a school, yes. And see if any fields could be put back into production again,' Penelope said. 'We'd also like to restore the manor house to live in when we're there. I do want you and Eleanor as neighbours so much.'

'Me and Eleanor?' he murmured, the last, most shining part of that envisaged puzzle sliding into enticing place.

Penelope smiled radiantly. 'Yes! Oh, I know it would all be rather easier with someone like Miss Evans at your side, but you *love* Eleanor. And she loves you. You deserve as much happiness as you can find for as many years as you may. You shouldn't have to wait so long for it as long as I have.' She smiled at Anthony.

Fred felt that glittering shard of hope grow, slowly. He hardly dared it might really happen. 'Pen, you are the best of friends, but I cannot take your money...'

Pen held up her hand, stopping his protest. 'I absolutely insist! You would never want to wound my feelings by refusing me this. I need to repay you and Eleanor for all your great kindness to me and now I am at last in a position to do so. I want happy homes for all of us, close to each other.'

Fred was utterly overwhelmed. His father had ruined them all and now they were helping each other to rebuild from such selfishness and bitterness. There was a justice in that. A joy. 'Very well, Pen. I know when I am outmanoeuvred.' He gave her an exuberant hug, the two of them laughing while crying with the new joy. 'You are the very finest of all stepmothers ever.'

Penelope giggled, and wiped away her tears. 'Ha! Now—you must sign this agreement and go and find Eleanor at once. You must cease your prowling about town. And shave before you leave.'

Fred laughed, and did exactly as she said. He signed—and dashed upstairs to shave and find his finest coat. He had one more, very important, piece of the happiness puzzle to find.

Chapter Seventeen

Eleanor hurried along the garden pathway, not seeing the flowers and hedges, the children dashing past with their hoops or the clouds sliding above. She only saw how it had all been the night of magical, other-worldly masquerade. The lanterns and pavilions and music. The hidden little summerhouse of such grand delights. She twisted Fred's handkerchief between her fingers as she walked, as a talisman.

Now, the world had righted itself, spinning them all back into their proper spots. Fred had to marry. She had to concentrate on her work. That was how it was always going to be. Surely it always was? So why did it now hurt so very much? Why did she feel as if the tether to the world itself was cut and she was floating along, unmoored and uncertain?

She turned a corner of the pathway, and headed towards the walkway beside the river. The crowds were thicker there. Couples arm in arm, nurses wheeling their elderly charges in their wicker bath chairs and children floating boats on the waves where Miss Muffins had once tumbled in. Laughter echoed from a Punch and Judy show.

But Eleanor couldn't feel the joyful scene at all. Couldn't feel the warmth of the sun. She wondered if she would ever find her centre again. Her joy in her work and duty. Her care and responsibility for everyone around her. Or if she would just drift up and up into the sky until she vanished alone.

Eleanor paused to open her parasol against the glow of the light. The flowers in the manicured beds seemed to shimmer, pinks, blues and yellows, and rays of silvery sunlight filtered through the leaves of the trees along the walkway. Two little children dashed past, shrieking, waving back at her.

She smiled wistfully. She'd never really envisaged her own family or children. There had been no time for such dreams. Not with the agency. Not with taking care of her sister and making certain they were secure. She made other peoples' happy futures. It had given her much pleasure to do that work, but lately sadness, wistfulness seemed to overtake her.

And now she couldn't even really help herself. She could not forget about Fred. Couldn't push the memories and hopes to the back of her mind as she had for so long. Fred was always right there. All these new, wild, passionate feelings overcoming her. She longed for him, so much. There was so much she could not have.

She'd thought surely the past would fade if she could see him again. She'd see he was no longer *her* Fred. That too much time had passed between them and too much change. But that summer-blue gleam of his beautiful eyes was just the same as it ever was. The laughter. The sense of fun. Pushed down but still there and still glorious. Eleanor barely saw his new scars.

She only ever saw Fred, her dear friend. The man she loved. The man whose kisses sent her spinning up like a firework. The man she wanted to talk to, walk with, kiss and laugh with for ever and ever. The man she wanted to share her work with and his with her. The man she wanted to help bring Moulton Magna back to its real glory and make it their real home. A place for their children.

Children! Eleanor's heart nearly burst at the thought. *Fred's* children.

She could just almost picture them. Blue eyes and golden hair. Or maybe her dark curls. She smiled to think of a blue-eyed little girl running through their own garden, shrieking in delight until Fred caught her up in his arms and tossed her up into the air amid wild laughter.

'*Mama, Mama, did you see?*' the girl would cry with a giggle.

It was so very much what Eleanor longed for now, had suppressed any thought of for so very long, and now here it was right in front of her. Reminding her of what she couldn't have. The agency was all she had now. She wouldn't jeopardise her livelihood. Her sister's livelihood! She would see Fred properly married and then she would forget him and go to the next patron and the next match. Fred would go back to Moulton Magna to set his own estate to rights and once he was out of sight one day he might also be out of mind.

Taking a deep breath, Eleanor turned sharply away from the scene and turned blindly along the river. She turned a corner towards a bridge—and froze. Miss Evans stood there, looking so young and beautiful and prosperous in pink silk and pearls with her glossy hair shining and her smile brilliant.

'M-Miss Evans,' Eleanor gasped. Miss Evans was surely the last person she wanted to see just then. Yet there she was, standing so close Eleanor couldn't run away.

'Miss Evans,' she said, curtsying with her most polite smile. Was it possible for a face to crack in half? 'How lovely to see you today. You are looking—very fine indeed.'

And she was. Miss Evans was always a pretty girl, but now there was a satisfaction in her eyes. A comfort in her eyes. A glow of happiness.

Happiness because of her new betrothal? Eleanor's heart ached and she feared she couldn't draw breath.

'How kind of you, Miss St Aubin! I feel well today indeed,' Miss Evans said with a laugh.

'Am I to wish you happy in your engagement?' Eleanor whispered. Her throat was so dry she could hardly say the words.

Miss Evans laughed again. Eleanor was sure it was the first time she'd heard such a sound from the solemn Miss Evans. 'Indeed you can wish me happy. For I am *not* to be married!'

Eleanor was bewildered. 'You are—not?'

'No! Luckily.' She linked arms with Eleanor and they strolled together beside the river path, past the

Punch and Judy show and the shrieking children. 'Your agency does splendid work, Miss St Aubin, you must not blame yourself in this instance. It is all *me*. I have never had the desire to marry, at least not yet, not until I am far into my botany studies.'

'You are a—botanist?' Eleanor whispered.

'Well—no. A mere amateur right now, but I wish with all my heart to make it my life's work. I may marry one day, if I'm fortunate enough to find a man who really understands. Perhaps even another scientist, so we could work together!'

'I shall keep an eye out for just such a man,' Eleanor said, bemused. Whatever she'd thought about Miss Evans, she'd never envisaged this—Miss Evans wanting to find her own path, a career. To do work she found important and maybe not to marry. Eleanor admired her greatly.

But—oh, what about Fred!

'Does Lord Fleetwood know?' Eleanor asked. 'The agency can certainly inform him, in the correct way, and find him another match.' Which would mean even more time spent close with Fred. Eleanor sighed in despair. Just when she had imagined it all over, she must begin again! Steel her heart again.

But then she realised—really and truly realised— Fred was *free*! He was not to marry Miss Evans. There would surely be talk about it all, Bath loved nothing more than gossip, but soon enough a new *on dit* would appear. It all seemed most amiable on Miss Evans' part.

Fred was free, but Moulton Magna was still in trouble.

'You have been such a friend, Miss St Aubin, truly,'

Miss Evans said. She kissed Eleanor's cheek and gave her a radiant smile. 'I shall never forget you.'

'And I shall look forward to seeing your beautiful work at Kew one day,' Eleanor answered.

Miss Evans squeezed her hands one more time and dashed away, no doubt thinking of plantings. Eleanor's head spun with all she had just heard. She turned away—and found Fred watching her.

She felt freezing and burning all at once. Her thoughts refusing to move. Not able to speak or walk or think. He wore no hat and his hair gleamed gold and copper in the sun. She started to run away.

'Ella! Wait!' he called.

Uncertain and all a tizzy, she half turned to leave, to flee. But Fred was quicker than her, even with his limp. He hurried through the crowd to her side. So close she smelled the lemony spicy Fred scent that always made her giddy.

He reached out his hand as if to touch her arm, but it fell away when she stepped back.

'Ella. How have you been?' he asked so carefully, almost as if they were strangers and he was wary of her. 'I tried to call, but Mary said you were unwell. I was rather worried.'

Eleanor forced herself to smile. 'Just a slight cold. I am quite well now.'

He nodded, a smile of relief on his lips. 'I was concerned you might hate me, after—well, after our last meeting.'

The meeting where he offered her all she had ever dreamed of. All she could never have. 'I couldn't hate you, Fred, not in a million years. You know that well. I was just—surprised, of course.' To put it mildly. 'And scared.'

'Scared of *me*?' he said, sounding most shocked.

'Not of you! How could I be scared of you, dearest Fred? My darling friend.'

'Then—what?'

'Scared of wanting too much, I suppose. Scared of that horrible, sharp disappointment when you must leave again. Any more goodbyes between us and it will become impossible to ever recover.'

He frowned and shook his head, as if he could not fathom her words. 'But that is the thing, Ella! We need never part again. It will be hard work, but if we were together...'

Eleanor was bewildered. 'What do you mean?

His frown suddenly transformed into a beam, like sunshine through a cloudy, obscuring grey sky. 'I mean we have such fine friends who wish to help us make a start and give us a chance to be together.'

'I am so confused, Fred. Tell me what is happening.'

Fred held out his arm to lead her along the river path. And there, amid the splash of the water, the ancient bridges crowded with parasols and laughing people and the leafy shadows of sunlight, he told her a fascinating tale. One hardly to be believed. One of Penelope and Anthony Oliver's rekindled romance. Of their buying the parcel of Moulton Magna land and building a school there. Of the chance to put the home farm into production and a roof on the house. All for friendship. All for love.

'So you see,' Fred finished as they came near the slippery bank where Miss Muffins once took her fateful tumble, 'The money from Mr Oliver and Pen opening the school, will give us the means we've needed to revitalise the estate or at least make a fine start. Of course we can't fix it all at once and it will mean a great deal of work. But I know we can do it. And in a year or two, we might even see a profit, with good luck and good weather. I will just need help, for I cannot do it all alone. And I know no one more organised and efficient and intelligent as my Ella. No one I want more by my side as we bring our home back to life. You know Moulton Magna, almost as well as I do. I am very sure between the two of us...'

It sounded amazing. A dream. Exactly what she'd always longed for. To have Fred and have useful work, too. Could she really do it? Dare to make that great leap?

'Fred,' she said slowly. 'I know Miss Evans is off on other endeavours now, but there are plenty of young ladies of fortune who would...'

'Ella!' He seized her hands, holding them tightly against his chest so she could feel the powerful beat of his heart. 'You could find me four hundred heiresses. A thousand! I would only ever want *you*. Your beauty and kindness and thoughtfulness. I need only you. Moulton Magna needs you.'

Eleanor felt the most glorious, sun-warm joy wash over her such as she had never known before. To have Fred and work, too! A home, one that wouldn't be taken from her as school and the vicarage had. To not worry about everything all the time any longer. To never have that sense of impermanence. To live a different life— one of happiness and purpose. It seemed…

'Wonderful,' she sighed.

His smile turned hopeful. 'Then you will marry me?'

Eleanor laughed, laughed longer and harder than she ever had in her life before. 'Yes! Yes, yes.' And she longed to dare to jump into his arms. But all those years of caution couldn't help but hold her back.

'What if…?' she began.

Fred shook his head. 'No what-ifs! Not any longer. This is at last our own moment. Yours and mine, Ella.'

Eleanor, dizzy and hopeful and sad all at the same time, took a step back. Her heel caught in the hem of her muslin skirt, throwing her off her balance.

The soles of her half-boots, slippery and thin, slid across the muddy ground and her arms flung out as if to grasp onto—nothing. Her parasol went flying. Icy panic flooded over her as she tumbled down towards the waiting water. Her cries made heads turn, alarmed onlookers came running, exclaiming. Surely this was just how Miss Muffins had felt!

'Ella!' Fred shouted, though she feared she was too far away for him to reach her in time. Her feet seemed to be suddenly made of glass. But Fred fooled them all. Sleek and swift as a tiger, just as she tumbled into the cold waves with a dramatic splash and squeezed her eyes shut, he lunged towards her and fell into the river with her. His firm arm around her waist kept her from sinking in her heavy skirts and pelisse and he pulled her from the brink and back onto solid ground.

The momentum of their weight sent him sliding backward, to land on his back on the bank with Eleanor atop him. For a moment they both lay very still, breathless and stunned.

Until Eleanor began shivering and applause broke out around them.

'So romantic…' a lady sighed.

Eleanor definitely knew then how Miss Muffins had felt. Like she was Fred's for ever.

He slowly sat up, drawing her with him. She found she quite lost any control then, sobbing in great gulps of relief and fear and love.

'We are safe now, my love,' he whispered, holding her close and wrapping his coat around her shoulders. 'Shh. I am here. I shall never leave you. I shall always make sure you're safe. Just as you have always saved me.'

'So we must always save each other,' she hiccuped. She very much liked the sound of that. She had always been the one to save others. Now he was there, with her, doing just the same for her.

'Always. We shall be the perfect team for ever.'

His lips claimed hers in a passionate kiss, warm and all-consuming, as the applause and cheers grew louder around them. Eleanor never wanted to let him go. And now she never had to. Happiness, giddy and free, flooded her heart and she dared kiss him again.

Fred laughed as they realised the avid attention all

around them. 'I see we are quite the *on dit*! I fear you must marry me now or cause a scandal.'

Eleanor reached up to hold his face tenderly between her hands and studied every angle and line of his beloved features. All the scars seemed vanished and he was only her golden Fred. 'Yes, Fred. I will marry you,' she said, just as she had dreamed of doing so very many times. But this was real. This was true. This was their whole life together. She went up on tiptoe, careless of the river puddle they stood in, and kissed him again and again, as if she would never cease.

Chapter Eighteen

A few months later

'**O**h, I do love a wedding day,' Eleanor declared, stretching luxuriously in the nest of sheets and blankets on her and Fred's rumpled honeymoon bed. She felt so warm, so tired and languid and perfect. 'And I have the feeling this wedding will be a particularly beautiful one!'

Fred laughed and burrowed deeper into the pillows beside her, burying his face in the loose fall of her hair. He gathered her closer and kissed her neck and bare shoulders until she giggled. 'Lovelier than our wedding?'

'Nothing could be lovelier than ours.'

White flowers and ribbons lining the altar. Rosy light streaming through the stained-glass window. Harry, Mary and Pen sniffling. Eleanor's new pale blue gown and veiled bonnet. Fred's hand in hers.

'But Pen's day will be just as beautiful. She deserves it so very much, after all she's been through. She and Anthony waited almost as long for each other as we did!'

And then, they would all travel to Moulton Magna to begin the hard work. To make a home. Surely the happiest home ever known. Mary and Harry would continue with the agency, of course. Mary was quite sure Mr Campbell needed a wife next.

'It's all too wonderful,' she sighed. 'Like a dream. I never want to wake up!'

'Beautiful Eleanor. My most glorious wife,' he said softly. He held her face gently between his large, callused palms as if she was the finest, most precious of delicate porcelain. A pearl beyond price. Despite their dozens of kisses, all the naughty, delicious things they'd devised to do together since they wed, every moment felt magical. Perfect. Like they had soared free of all the worries that held them apart far too long and burst free into the heavens together.

Clinging to each other, they fell back to the rumpled bed. The painted mural on the ceiling, of gods and goddesses and cupids in their filmy draperies and laurel wreaths, whirled around their heads dizzily. Eleanor spun on top of her husband, not able to breathe as she studied him in the first sunrise light filtering through the windows. His bare skin seemed gilded with the amber-tinged glow and his battle scars were hidden. How glorious he was. Vibrant and glowing with strength and with raw desire that burned in his eyes. How could he be hers now at long last? It was beyond any of her old dreams.

Her trailing fingertips traced the light, coarse sprinkling of dark gold hair on his naked chest and the thin line that arrowed enticingly to the band of his loosened breeches. His stomach muscles tightened and his breath went raged and harsh as her touch brushed across his skin.

'Ella, my darling,' he gasped. 'Be careful. If you're sore from last night…'

Eleanor laughed to remember the long, glorious night. Three times!

'I am perfectly well. If *you* have the strength.' She smiled as she touched every last, warm, silken inch of him. Yes, *this*—this was the most right thing she had ever done. The exact place she most wanted to be.

She fell back into his arms, their lips meeting, heartbeats melding as one. There was no longer anything careful, cautious about their kisses. They were as hot as the sun and filled with an urgent deep need, like the fireworks that once burst over Sydney Gardens. She felt the heat of his hands as he slid her light, silk nightdress from her shoulders and she pushed it away with no shyness at all.

'Ella,' he groaned, his hands tightening on her hips, so warm and strong. 'So very beautiful.'

How she hoped she *was* beautiful now, for him. Her husband, her only love. She kissed him again and he rolled her body beneath his, across their tangled sheets.

She laughed as her hair spilled all around them. She certainly did feel beautiful as he looked at her. She felt free at last. Burst out of responsibility and propriety and expectations. Only with him. There was only now, this one moment, where she was with the husband she loved. He kissed her and all other thoughts vanished.

She closed her eyes and let herself revel in the feeling his touch created. The press of his lips on her bare skin. Her palms slid over his back. So strong. So hot. Slick with sweat and sheltering her with all his strength. Her legs parted as she felt his weight lower between them and press forward to make them one.

'My beautiful Ella,' he gasped.

Slowly, so slowly, he moved again within her. Drawing back. Edging forward. A little deeper and more intimate each time. Ella closed her eyes, feeling all the ache and stretch ebb away until there was only that pleasure she had come to crave. A tingling delight that grew and expanded inside of her heart, exploding like the fireworks of the masquerade. Before Fred, she'd never imagined anything as wondrous at all.

She cried out at the wonder of it all, at the bursts of light behind her closed eyes, all blue and white gold. The heat of it was too much. How could she survive without being consumed with him to nothing?

Above her, all around her, she felt his body grow taut and his back arch. 'Ella!' he shouted out.

She utterly flew apart, clinging to him as she let herself fall down into that fire and be happily consumed.

After long, slow moments she blinked her eyes open, wondering if they had somehow tumbled into a deep volcano. But it was just their bed, the white sanctuary they had barely left since their wedding. Yet that wonderful sparkle still clung to her.

Collapsed beside her on the pillows, his arms tight around her, was her Fred. Her husband. He seemed to be asleep. His breath harsh. Limbs sprawled out in exhaustion. His hair was bright in the new daylight.

His face smooth and young as he had not been in so very long.

Eleanor smiled at the sight, like the painted Mars collapsed exhausted next to Botticelli's rather smug Venus, and she felt herself floating ever so slowly back to earth. Morning was even more glorious than she had ever dreamed. She always became someone different in his arms. Someone beautiful and bold and free. And she revelled in it all.

The ormolu clock on the mantel chimed, dropping her fully back to earth and reminding her where they were really were. What time it really was.

Eleanor sat up bolt-straight on the bed and reached for her wrinkled gown. 'Fred! We must hurry.'

'Why?' he groaned, muffled in his pillow. 'I'm happy right here.'

'As am I. But if we don't rush, we shall be late for Pen's wedding. And that would never do!'

She slid out of bed and hurried to the windows to pull the draperies open. The spires of the Abbey sparkled and crowds already hurried over the cobblestones. Shops were opening. Flower carts appearing. 'Happy is the bride the sun shines upon!'

Fred propped himself up on his elbow to watch her with a bemused grin on his morning-whiskers face. 'It rained on our wedding day.'

Ella laughed to think of it. The grey skies that had done nothing to dampen her joy, even if it had somewhat wilted her new hat.

'And also happy the bride the rain blesses! It will mean a fine harvest next year at Moulton Magna.' She kissed him quickly and tossed him his dressing gown. 'Happy every bride who loves her bridegroom. That is the only thing that really matters.'

'And Pen loves Oliver?'

Eleanor smiled to think of how Pen and Anthony secretly held hands all the time. How they smiled at each other, staring into each other's eyes. 'Assuredly. And this is going to be the most beautiful of days. Now— get dressed! There's not much time…'

'There! I think we have done quite a fine job here, don't you?' Mary said as she straightened the pearl-pinned flowers in Penelope's curls.

'You have indeed!' Penelope answered, turning her head one way then the other to study the effect of the white blooms against her dark hair and the gleaming pearl earrings that were the groom's wedding gift. The pale pink gown with its antique lace trim, the large bouquet of roses and lilies—both like something in a fairy tale story. Like a queen's wedding, mayhap. A queen who loved her prince.

So different from her first two weddings. Not least because of the new happy glow in her eyes.

Harry fastened the last detail around Penelope's neck, a triple-stringed pearl necklace clasped with a massive ruby. One more surprise last-minute gift from Anthony. 'There. Perfect.'

There was a knock at the chamber door and Eleanor appeared, holding Natalie and Grace by their little hands. They bounced excitedly on their slippered toes in their yellow and white bridesmaids' dresses and wreaths of flowers around their heads.

'I think all is in readiness now, Pen.'

'The carriage is waiting to take you on your honeymoon!' Natalie burst out. 'And it's *covered* with flowers!'

Eleanor laughed. 'I am sure every florist shop is quite empty in Bath.'

Penelope laughed, too. She carefully touched one dark curl, feeling a sudden touch of chill. 'Am I really entirely worthy of him, do you think, my dears?'

Mary grabbed her gloved hand. 'You two have been waiting for each other for years and years, my dear! Now you get to claim your prize. No one deserves perfect happiness more than you and Anthony.'

Penelope laughed again, this time filled with joy, half coughing with happy tears. 'And Ella and Fred!'

'And look at how disgustingly happy they are,' Harry said. 'We shall all be quite tired of hearts and flowers soon.'

'Until you find your own perfect knight.' Penelope rose from the dressing table and made her slow way down the stairs, Natalie and Grace carrying her lace-edged train. More flowers twined the banisters and waited below. Scenting the air like it was July at Kew Gardens. She could hear the faint strains of harp music, murmurs and laughter.

Her bridegroom waited in the drawing room, for the small ceremony a special licence had granted them. There, in the beam of sunlight before the makeshift altar of a lace-draped buffet table and silver vases of roses, she glimpsed that dashing young man who once so enraptured her. The man she'd thought she couldn't have. The man who had shown her the joy and fun of life.

She'd never dared dream they could be here now, together. And there he was. Hers.

She made her way up the Aubusson carpet aisle, smiling at her friends gathered there between the flowers. Mary, Charles Campbell, Adele, Harry, Miss Evans, Eleanor and Fred. Once, she could never have imagined so much happiness in one place. And now it was theirs. For ever.

She reached out for Anthony's hand, smiled and blessed all that Bath had brought them.

* * * * *

*While you're waiting for the next book in
Amanda McCabe's Matchmakers of Bath miniseries
why not check out her recent Historical romances?*

'A Convenient Winter Wedding'
in *A Gilded Age Christmas*
A Manhattan Heiress in Paris

Or fall in love with any of her Dollar Duchesses in
His Unlikely Duchess
Playing the Duke's Fiancée
Winning Back His Duchess